SPEAKING OUT

Black Girls in Britain

Audrey Osler

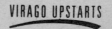

VIRAGO UPSTARTS

Published by VIRAGO PRESS Limited 1989
20–23 Mandela Street, Camden Town, London NW1 0HQ

*A CIP catalogue record for this book
is available from the British Library*

Typeset by Centracet, Cambridge
Printed in Great Britain
by Guernsey Press Ltd, C.I.

CONTENTS

▪▪▪▪▪▪▪▪▪▪▪▪▪▪▪▪▪▪▪▪▪▪▪▪▪▪▪▪▪▪▪▪▪▪▪▪▪▪▪

To my mother, Esmé

Acknowledgements

This book has been written with the help and support of many people, in particular, the sixteen girls who talked to me about their lives, thoughts and feelings. Without your contributions, enthusiasm and encouragement, the book could not have been written. I enjoyed working with you.

I am also grateful for the support of many others: the headteachers and teachers who gave me access to their schools and helped arrange meetings with girls. Edwina Cook and Elizabeth Fullbrook for transcribing many hours of tape. Colleagues at Birmingham Development Education Centre for giving me time and flexibility. The good friends who have helped by discussing the project; criticizing the text; and providing encouragement: especially John Hopkin, Christel Mertens and Clare Simmonds. Many thanks to you all.

Introduction:
Making our voices heard

■■

'Girls must learn to stand up for themselves, whether they are
Asian, Afro-Caribbean, English or whatever. It doesn't really
matter who you are, what matters is to spend time talking
about what you want to do. Although we've found out that
we've got the same kind of ideas on many issues I was
surprised and impressed by what the others said. I'm glad we
got together and had this sort of talk.'

This is how Afia, one of the sixteen girls whose views are
represented in *Speaking Out*, summed up her feelings about
taking part. When I decided to write this book and to interview
groups of Black girls in Birmingham, I felt that it was about
time that people had the chance to hear what Black girls and
young women had to say about life, and about their own lives in
particular.

Like most of the girls in *Speaking Out* I was born in this
country and went to school here. My mother is from Singapore
and my father is English. I am very interested in my family
history and proud of my descent but have felt shocked and
angry when other people have interpreted my identity for me. I
have shared some of the experiences and feelings of the girls in
this book and felt it was important that they should have the
opportunity to speak out for themselves.

When I started work as a teacher I soon found out that there
is plenty to read about the experiences and needs of Black
students but it is hard to find very much written by the students
themselves. Black girls' views are rarely sought but other people

are often ready to make huge assumptions and generalizations about our hopes and futures. These people include many who make decisions which affect the lives of Black girls and young women. It was for these reasons that I invited three groups of Black girls to share their ideas on a number of subjects. I hope that other students, parents and teachers will listen to what they have to say about their lives.

I visited three secondary schools and talked to girls in the fourth year, aged fourteen and fifteen. All the girls went to school in the Birmingham area. Some attended a school where Black students were in a minority, others were in schools where they formed a majority. Four went to a girls' school. Each group met about once a week over a period of six months and the girls discussed various aspects of their lives, such as the city they lived in; their friends and families; their hopes for the future; and their views on other parts of the world. At the end of the series of group discussions each girl had the opportunity to talk on her own about any of these subjects.

The girls knew that the purpose of the discussions was to provide material for this book. Many of the girls wished their identities, their families and their schools to remain private, and for this reason the names of all who took part have been changed as have some details of where they live. At the beginning of each chapter individual girls are introduced.

Throughout this book I have used the term 'Black' to refer to people of Afro-Caribbean and Asian descent in Britain. The girls tend to use the term in the same way, but where there is a need to refer specifically to one or other of the two groups they often use 'Black' to refer to Afro-Caribbean people only. There is of course a wide variety of cultures, religions and languages within the two groups. To use the term 'Black' to describe people of both Afro-Caribbean and Asian descent is not to deny the many differences which exist not only between the communities but also within them. Yet this does not prevent people from making generalizations about Asian or Afro-Caribbean people, often from a racist standpoint. Self-identity is very important; people may prefer to describe themselves according to their religion, ethnic group or country of origin.

There are many reasons for using one term to describe people of such varied cultures and for choosing to write jointly about the experiences of girls of Asian and Afro-Caribbean descent. Much of what has been written about Black girls has been written in terms of problems. Black people are seen to be difficult because they have not accepted white cultural values. Young Black people are often viewed as a problem for their schools, for teachers, for the police, for social workers, and for white society generally. The very real problem for Black people of living in a racist society is often overlooked.

Race issues are significant in determining the day-to-day experiences of Black girls in Britain, as are those of gender and class. In *Speaking Out* girls from a variety of different cultures within the Afro-Caribbean and Asian communities have had a chance to discuss these experiences together. Despite differences of opinion and of cultural background, everyone had the experience of what it is like to be a Black girl growing up in Britain. This experience gives all the voices in *Speaking Out* a common perspective.

The girls in this book are not intended to be typical representatives of their various cultures, but to reflect something of the range of cultures which can be found within the Black British community. Their experience is that of living in a large multi-racial city, Birmingham. Birmingham has about one million inhabitants, about a quarter of whom are of Afro-Caribbean or Asian descent. The total number of Black or bilingual pupils in Birmingham schools can only be estimated as statistics have never been collected on a city-wide basis. The highest estimates are about one third of the total.

Many of the issues which are important to Black girls are also of importance to white girls, and white girls reading *Speaking Out* will easily recognize this, but they will also encounter some vast differences in experience. Erica expressed it like this:

3

'We talk about Black girls and white girls, but it's not as though we're two different species. Of course we feel the same things as each other, it's just that in some situations Black girls have had different things happen to them and work against them. There will be other situations where this has happened to white girls.'

The girls I talked to in this book often assumed sexism as an almost inevitable part of their experience. In some cases, they were ready to challenge this sexism at home, at school and elsewhere in society, but for most, it was racism which caused greater anger and pain and which led to greater resistance.

When I first had the idea of writing *Speaking Out* I felt strongly that what Black girls in Britain have to say would be important and challenging to many people. Many of the girls I spoke to told me that some of the things they included in our conversations they would find hard or even impossible to say in front of white people. Some felt that their parents would not have been able to recognize them from what they were saying. For others, our conversations gave them a new opportunity to hear each other's opinions and to discover that other Black girls felt the same way about things.

As we talked together I discovered for myself new courage and hope in the strength of these young Black women and in what they have to say both about growing up in Britain today and about their lives and futures.

The Girls

■■

Here is a brief note about each of the characters in *Speaking Out*. Individual girls are introduced more fully at the beginning of each chapter.

Angela hopes to become an engineer, or failing that, a top hair stylist. Her family are from Jamaica.

Jasbir is from a strict Sikh family, but is anxious to point out that each Asian family is different. She wants to be a photographer.

Satnam hopes to become a nursery nurse. Her family are Sikhs and she feels angry about the way the Sikh community is portrayed in the media.

Nazrah is a Muslim and she's very keen on sport. At the time of the interviews she was looking forward to moving to Pakistan with her family.

Anita takes life quite seriously and describes herself as a sort of socialist. Her ambition is to study law at university. Her family are from India.

Pauline is from a Rastafarian family, and since childhood she has wanted to become a nurse or doctor.

Erica would eventually like to live in America. Her parents are from Jamaica. She likes going out to nightclubs with her friends.

Arina is very sociable and her ambition is to travel. Her mother is from Bangladesh and her father was a Trinidadian Asian. The family are Muslims.

Elaine is interested in history and politics, particularly in Northern Ireland and South Africa. Her mother is English and her father is from Jamaica.

Afia is a Muslim. She plans to go to art college and to become a fashion designer.

Marcia is a keen netball and volleyball player. Her ambition is to be an accountant or a solicitor and to prove that Black women can succeed. Her parents are from Jamaica.

Gillian is a member of a swimming club and spends a lot of her time training. She would like to be a probation officer or social worker. Her family are from Jamaica.

Tara is a Hindu and has fond childhood memories of a holiday in India. She'd very much like to travel and thinks she may become an air stewardess.

Rasheeda is engaged to her cousin in Pakistan. The family are Muslims. She is determined to complete her education and establish herself in a career before she marries.

Mumtaz sees her future here in Britain and is studying hard with the aim of taking up a legal career. Her family, who are Muslims, are very close and give her lots of support.

Cynthia has been brought up in a strict Christian family. Her parents are from Jamaica. Cynthia's ambition is to become an actress.

1:
School:
It's not fair!

■■■

Anyone who has been through school will have had, at one time or another, the feeling that 'It's not fair!'

A lot is written in the newspapers about inner-city schools. How much of it is true? Does school treat girls fairly? Research has shown that girls can be extremely disadvantaged at school, but there is little to read about the differing experiences of Black girls and white girls. Are Black girls succeeding or failing? Is school providing them with a full range of choices and opportunities?

Education has long been an issue of much concern within the Black community in Britain. Parents have responded to inadequate schools by setting up alternative classes and schools for their children. For the majority of students these classes do not provide a complete solution. How then are Black girls responding to these problems? Two of the girls who participated in this discussion were Angela and Jasbir.

Angela

Angela was born in Moseley, Birmingham and now lives in Erdington. Her parents are both from Jamaica, her mother from Clarendon and her father from St Catherine.

Angela's parents have talked to her a good deal about their lives in Jamaica and about their early experiences in Britain. Her mother came as a schoolgirl of thirteen, arriving with her parents. Her grandparents have mixed feelings about moving to Britain:

Angela's grandad is a tailor, but here he has never really been able to charge people a realistic fee for his skills. He has also suffered ill health since settling in Britain.

Angela's father came to Britain as a young man of twenty-three. He was keen to travel and came looking for better job opportunities in Britain. He found a job in a car factory. Angela's mother left school at fifteen and started work in a clothing factory. She then taught herself to type, and while working, studied to become a librarian, which is what she now works as.

'I have a good relationship with my parents but my mum doesn't let me get away with anything. She says that she wants me to come out of school with a good education and she wants me to pass all my exams. It's important that I get the main ones like maths and English. My parents wouldn't mind me going to university, but I don't expect to get that far. They want me to go to college and study hard and pass, then after that I can get a good job.'

Angela's ambition is to become an engineer or a mechanic, but she worries that she won't make it in her chosen career, partly because of male opposition and partly through her own lack of confidence. She says hairdressing would be her second choice.

Angela enjoys a number of sports including badminton, tennis, weight-training and sprinting. She also likes dancing and occasionally goes to nightclubs with her friends.

She would like to live in London, where she has family. She says she feels happier there than in Birmingham. Angela is also keen to travel and sees herself as advantaged in having family in different parts of the world.

'I've got family all over; in London, Canada, Jamaica, America and Trinidad. You get a better idea of what other countries are like, and more opportunities for travelling. I think I'm lucky because if my parents had been brought up here then I don't think I'd know much about Jamaica.'

Jasbir

Jasbir's family are Sikhs. Her mother was brought up in Kenya and went to live in India, where she married Jasbir's father. From India they moved to England and the family finally settled in Edgbaston.

The family have recently moved house and Jasbir's grandmother has come to live with them. Jasbir has a sister who is about a year older than her, and a much younger brother and sister. Her father works for West Midlands Transport and her mother is a machinist who takes in sewing at home.

The family spend most of their time together and Jasbir and her sister enjoy the company of their cousins who live nearby. They travel regularly to London to spend weekends with other members of the family. Jasbir has very little personal freedom and is expected to stay at home and help with the cooking, housework and care of the younger children, something which she resents very much; she says: 'Our parents are really strict, and when we've got our granny with us they're twice as strict.' Jasbir's ambition is to be a photographer; her cousin who lives in London has supported her in this. Unfortunately her parents disapprove of the idea, and of the cousin, and are unwilling for her to take up any work which may involve her moving away from home. They feel that if she is not going to continue studying then she should get married as soon as possible. Jasbir is very much against this, and often finds herself in confrontation with her parents.

Jasbir would very much like to visit India. She first went when she was about four years old, but can remember very little of that experience.

The girls chose to talk about changing attitudes of Black students towards school and how school treats Black girls. Girls often find themselves stereotyped, and schools may expect Black girls and their parents to conform to a number of limited patterns. The girls had strong feelings about ways schools could change to meet Black students' needs.

White school, Black students

Marcia
'Education is becoming less of a problem for Black people. About five years ago I might have said that poor schools might have been one of the reasons for the troubles in Handsworth, but nowadays I don't think schools can be blamed. In one Handsworth school they've had projects on the local community and studied the cause of the riots. That's only one school, not all, but it's a good move.

'Schools have changed. They've realized certain things were happening to Black pupils and things have changed for the better. They respect Black pupils more. I can think of one school where they don't really like Blacks or Asians, but most schools are coming to terms with things, and respecting their pupils more. They see Black kids not as something unfortunate but as people, and as important as everyone else. They recognize that Black pupils have got a brain and everything. Now they're beginning to treat everyone as equal.'

Turning the other cheek

Marcia
'Black people are looking at themselves now. People are realizing that if they want to get somewhere in this world they have got to get out and do it, not mess around. People are changing their attitudes towards school.'

Gillian

'It's not only in school that Black and Asian are starting to say "I'm not going to take that anymore. I'm going to stand up to anybody that gives me hassle." I've seen it done. In the early days people were turning the other cheek. Now Asian and Black people are saying they haven't got another cheek to turn. They've been turned too many times.'

Race, gender, and class – making the links

Elaine

'Black people are often put back and even white girls don't always do so well. Black working-class girls are often in the worst position. But that doesn't mean they do worst, it means they try harder. I don't think that's always the case because in this school I've always had a fair chance. It's always seemed fair to me, but I'm the only Black girl in the top class.'

Gillian

'When you start school at eleven they put you into groups. At the end of the third year they rearrange things and put you into options. I've seen a lot of people, both Black and white, from lower classes than me doing better than me once we were mixed for options. But there were always more Black people in the lower streams. You thought people were less clever, and then you find you've been proved wrong – some of the cleverest have been in the bottom classes.'

Cynthia

'I agree with that. From the start they should have put us into mixed groups and we could then see how everybody could have grown and grown. If they put you in a low class, as they did with me, then the teachers assume that you're not going to be clever. They think, "Cynthia is never going to do well." But if

I'd been in a mixed class teachers would accept me and recognize me for what I am.'

Afia
'I think that England is really behind in education and it's getting worse thanks to the government's policies on education. Baker brings up new policies every day and he hasn't even thought about them. He has no idea what schools are like. He says, "We're going to do this today" and then the next day, "We're going to do this". He just doesn't think about what he's said. He's just throwing out one idea after another.'

Strong language

A large proportion of Black students are bilingual, but instead of regarding this as an advantage, many teachers and schools still refer to their developing bilingual students as 'those who can't speak English properly'. At secondary school their bilingualism often becomes totally hidden. Students are rarely encouraged to use their home or community languages in class, and may choose not to in the playground for fear of being mocked. Often the other students and teachers may be unaware of the languages spoken by particular students and will have difficulty in actually naming them.

Rasheeda
'When girls speak their own language, the English girls look down on them. I don't think that's right because we should be able to speak whatever language we want. When the French come on exchanges and speak their language they're not looked down upon. We should feel free to speak our language. After all, we learn languages at school. Some learn Spanish and French, so why not Urdu or Punjabi? I think it should be so.'

Nazrah

'If people are talking French, English girls don't mock them. They may sometimes do impersonations of French people talking fast, but that's as far as it goes. They don't look down on the French, they look up to them, they think they're gods. English girls come in wearing their best skirts, their best frocks, mainly because of the French boys, thinking they're romantic. In fact they're nothing like it, they're really rude. But it's the way they're seen.'

Afia

'When we had Urdu introduced into our school a few years back most people thought it would be a failure and that nobody would take it. People thought of it as a useless language, but it's really helpful for Asian girls. There are lots of us and I think we should know our language. As with all languages you learn about the country's background and that's important to us as well. But a lot of people were upset when they saw Urdu signs, and pictures to do with Asian things stuck up on the walls. They were saying, "Why have them? They could corrupt." They were saying that it's a waste, arguing that it's a load of rubbish. They were frightened.'

It was pointed out that people used to have similar attitudes when Black people spoke Patois:

Marcia

'At one time they would have been saying "What are you saying? Speak English." But nowadays people like the Patois and lots of white people want to speak it. They're always asking, "How do you say this in Patois? How do you say that?" Years ago they would have said, "Get back to your own country. You can't even speak English." They would have degraded you and your language.'

Angela

'Some white girls, if they mix with Black girls enough, they can talk Patois like us. People might say, "Oh look, she thinks she's Black" but they like to learn how we talk. I talk Patois to my friends, and a white girl, Tracey, she talks it to me! She's really good, she makes me laugh, and I like her for that. Considering she's just picked it up from us she's very good. I think white girls and Black girls should get together more and talk about how they feel.'

Learning to survive: parents and school

Mumtaz

'My dad thinks we should get a good education and go to the highest level that we can. Our family is on its own in Britain with no other relations here. I don't think we're ever going back to Pakistan, at least not until we grow really old. We're going to live here so we should try to make ourselves as comfortable as we can. He's always telling us how hard it was back in Pakistan and how hard he had to work just to come to England and set up home here. That makes us determined to work hard to satisfy our parents that they've brought us up for something good.'

One girl received particular encouragement from her mother because her mother's own experience of school in Britain was not good:

Angela

'My mother went to a girls' school in Birmingham and she left when she was fifteen and went straight to work in a clothing factory. She studied typing and word processing and then she studied literature and so on, and became a librarian. She said she enjoyed school in Jamaica better, because over here they weren't so strict. Over there they made people work hard, but over here they didn't seem to take much notice or care about their work.

At my school things are better. There are different races and mostly we all get on in the school. There's no problem about the teachers picking on us.'

The other girls from the same school tended to agree, but they qualified this:

Pauline
'Sometimes they are expecting trouble from us before they have got to know us properly.'

Arina
'If you're Asian or Black they think you probably won't know much. They choose you for particular things.'

'Good at sport' or 'Shy and stupid'

Erica
'They definitely choose Black people for sport. They think it just comes naturally or something like that. If they want someone to represent the school for something else they'll choose a white girl or a white boy.'

Anita
'They expect Asian girls to be quiet and not very clever. When you try and prove them wrong they'll just say, "She's a loud mouth!" It takes time before they accept you.'

Equal opportunities?

At Nazrah's school the girls felt that despite the headteacher's belief in equality for all races, in practice the school remained racist because of the attitudes of many of the girls and some of the teachers:

Nazrah
'Whites always have first opportunities and they always come first whatever. I think there should be equal opportunities.

It was chemistry. I was singing an Asian song with a friend, and my best friend – she's Afro-Caribbean – said, "Don't tell me you're one of those?" I said to her, "One of what?" She replied, "You know, TP" and I asked her, "What's TP?" She said, "Typical Paki". I answered her, "So what, I'm proud of what I am." She said, "I know you are." And then I said to her, "Just because I wear these clothes (a skirt and blouse) doesn't mean I'm walking away from our flag. I'm not antagonistic to my own culture."'

Dress sense

Mumtaz
'Most of the girls at this school wear Asian dress, and when I came here my mum told me, "You can wear Asian dress if you want to, you can choose what to wear." But the white girls here when they see a girl in Asian clothes they think, "Oh no, she's a typical Paki, she's one of those who doesn't know anything, she must be in the bottom class." So I thought I'd better wear the uniform.'

Rasheeda
'Sometimes you will see a teacher let Asian girls sit there and get on with their work and not try to involve them in class

discussions. This seems to happen to girls who are dressed in traditional Asian clothes.'

Whose country is it, anyway?

Afia
'The head announced in assembly that the local council was giving leaders in the Pakistani community some money to finance an anniversary. Afterwards as I walked up the corridor I overheard two girls in our class saying to each other, "Who do these Pakis think they are? They're taking over our country and they're taking our money." But when they saw me they went very quiet. I asked, "What are you saying?" and they answered, "Oh, nothing!" and left it at that. But there are other girls in our class and they just tell you out straight. I think that's wrong because we live here so we've got to have our celebrations like they have Christmas and Easter and so on. They spend loads of money on those so I don't see why we shouldn't.

'Another time our head encouraged people to do projects on Pakistan. Most English girls responded with "Oh, this is typical. She just wants the Asians doing something." There were prizes given out and they were demanding, "They're doing projects on Pakistan, why not on Britain?" But we do Britain in History, we do it everywhere, it touches the whole of our lives; it's nice to have something different to do. White girls came to me and they asked, "Are you doing that project on Pakistan?" I wasn't because I had too much homework to do, so I told them I wasn't. They said, "Oh, that's all right then." They thought that whoever was doing the project on Pakistan was a "Typical Paki" and absolutely dumb.'

Who benefits?

Marcia

'In geography we normally do things about earthquakes and things like that. Even when we look at food, rice for example, we never really learn about people. We had one teacher who talked about relationships between countries and about trade. We learnt about the export of bananas from Jamaica and who benefits and grows rich and who loses out. We shared out the money, each of us taking the part of real people. Now that was really good.

'The thing that surprised me was that people didn't even know the basic facts: they were surprised to find out that bananas come from Jamaica; that we import them from there; and that they grow on trees. But they were interested, asking lots of questions because it was linked in with their own lives.'

Anita

'When I was little I used to think that Britain, America and Japan were the only sort of civilizations and that all the other people used to run around in grass skirts and things like that. That's how I used to think, and I guess something in my childhood, in my primary school or whatever, gave me that impression. Even though my parents came from India I still had this view of India. I thought, "Oh, they just live in little villages and straw huts."'

Angela

'In schools they may not do it consciously but they help form your impressions. When you do geography you do the geography of Africa. They don't talk about the cities, they talk about the little villages and how ten people live in one little hut. If you travel you find out that's not true. Of course some people live in villages, but there are modern places as well.

They call them the "Third World" countries. Why can't they just call them countries?'

Jasbir
'We know more about other countries than most white girls, because for a start we know about our own countries, the countries where our parents are from. I know a bit about India. Because of who you are, you learn more from your parents and from other friends. You get all your information like that.'

Drugs, alcohol or religion

Cynthia
'If you're studying R.E. you want to learn about religion, about everybody's religion. I've never come across an R.E. lesson since the third year that was anything to do with religion. Before that it was just Christianity, and now it's drugs, alcohol, unmarried mothers, abortion or divorce. Everything but religion!'

Marcia
'I think that was because our R.E. teacher wasn't all that good. I talked to him and I asked him why we hadn't covered more about different religions. He told me he hadn't really studied them and that he couldn't really go into them because he would have to guess a bit and would not really know any of the facts. So he only knew about Jesus Christ, but not about Muslims or Sikhs or anyone else. So that's why we were covering little bits about drugs and so on. He wasn't all that well prepared.'

Jasbir
'I had an Asian R.E. teacher at my last school, and that was much better. Being in England she has to cover Christian religion, and coming from another country she can understand

other religions too. She knows more than just about her own country. She's bound to learn about the English because she lives here. It's the same for us. We know about English people because we live here. But what do they know about us?'

Whose history?

Afia
'We know a lot more about white people than they know about us because we're living in their society. All you are learning is their history and they don't learn about our history. In school we only learn about other countries' histories when they affected British history. You learn it from the British point of view so you don't learn anything outside British history.'

Satnam
'All of us put together probably know a lot more than some of the teachers. I know quite a bit about India from what I pick up at home. My parents and family are always talking about it.'

Tara
'I know a bit about the Hindu gods and things like that. I don't know a lot, but I don't think an ordinary teacher would know anything about it.'

Elaine
'My dad came over to this country when he was about eleven and he never really tells me about Jamaica, but I've wanted to find out about my background so I've learnt about it myself. I've learnt about South Africa myself because I know it's a waste of time waiting for the teachers to say anything about it.'

Books are dangerous!

Marcia
'I find out what I want to know from books, but there is a problem with most books when they show Black children. They're shown to be all poor. And they don't show the rich parts of Asia or Africa, it's the same on telly. They do exactly the same thing.'

Arina
'White people think of Black people and they get their ideas from books. They give little children books with golliwogs and monkeys, and then they turn round and call you "black monkey" or "black golliwog"! Is it surprising? They get it from the books!'

Cynthia
'In Rosa Guy's books she shows an upper class and a poor girl as well. We have never studied her in school, but I came across her one day in the school holidays when I was watching a programme. Rosa Guy was sitting in a group of kids and they were discussing a book. Some Black actresses and actors did a part from one of her books. I'd really like to study more Black authors and Asian literature as well.'

Gillian
'In the third year we studied *My Mate Shofiq* [by Jan Needle] and there were loads of white kids in our class and they were all making fun of the way the family lives. Laughing at the way the mother stays at home most of the time and everything like that. But the teacher talked about why they were calling her names, about being "slagged off" because of who you are. If you're Pakistani, they cut the word to "Paki" and it's an insult. And

Black, they change that to "blackie" and it amounts to the same.'

Marcia

'But that's because we had Miss B for English in the third year and she's not frightened to talk about these things. We read *Roll of Thunder, Hear My Cry* by Mildred Taylor and I thought the book was really interesting. I had to go and get the sequel, *Let the Circle Be Unbroken*. It's about Black Americans. The Black woman in the story, she was good. She really summed up everyone's feelings. It was set just after slavery days and showed how the white people treated the Black people. It really dealt with racism and showed a Black girl standing up for her rights. But most teachers are reluctant to discuss these kinds of things. It's guilt.'

Pauline

'The English books we read in school, they're mostly white people's books. They may be interesting, but to me they are not as interesting as books about Black people. Rosa Guy is one of my favourite authors. I've read all her books. She's Black and her books are based on the lives of Black people.'

Girls only!

Afia and some of the other girls attended a single-sex school. It is sometimes argued that girls tend to do better at a girls' school, and that Asian girls, and Muslim girls in particular, often prefer this type of education. Anita described some of the problems she had encountered in a mixed school.

Anita

'In the second and third year you have to choose from a number of craft options: home economics, technical drawing, needlework, and so on. I put my name down for craft and design. I never got it, I got put in a needlework class. It could have been because the class was full up but I don't really think so. It was probably because I was a girl. There's no real excuse. When there are only ten or twelve people in a craft and design class it could hold more. They gave the options to the boys. The needlework class is full and there are no boys. Maybe some of them chose to do needlework. I think in reality the choices were made for you. It was on the top of the form showing you can choose but the choices were made for you.'

Mumtaz
'In school we have Life Skills, and they've taught us some of our rights. The teachers are usually women and so we've looked at the rights of rape victims, for example, but racism, we didn't cover that at all. It would have been good if we did. You should have a subject where you cover these everyday kind of things. I think it would help.'

But there are also disadvantages in single-sex girls' schools:

Afia
'Women could do a lot more for women and school could help. They could put more subjects in. There's nothing here like woodwork or mechanics. From a sexist point of view it's all girls' stuff. We need more of what we are going to face when we go into the outside world. We've got commerce but only a few people are allowed to do that. We should have business studies for everybody and opportunities to experience a greater variety of things before we leave school.

'I think that women should start a lot of businesses and employ more women instead of men. That way they would build up the position of women and so make women more confident in their line of work. If some started that, with small firms which would grow bigger, then all women could gain confidence from them.

'Just because some women achieve important positions doesn't mean that it's got any easier for women. We've got a woman Prime Minister but you can't really say that she has done anything to help other women. I suppose something is achieved if people think of the Prime Minister as "she" as well as "he", but Margaret Thatcher as a person hasn't done anything to make women's lives any better. In fact she's made things a lot more difficult for many people, especially women, who are much more hard up.'

2:
Black teachers:
white school

There is no reason to suspect that Birmingham schools are overall any better or worse in their treatment of Black students than those in other areas. Birmingham students are probably no more or less affected by racism than any others. Of course there are likely to be differences between schools. Perhaps one of the most obvious is in the attitudes of the teachers.

In one secondary school where the majority of the students were Black a white teacher would happily talk about the 'right' colour and the 'wrong' colour and could regularly get away with racist remarks in the staffroom. He was a senior member of staff and none of his white colleagues chose to challenge him. I did not interview any girls there, but this happened to be a school with a reputation for 'good multicultural education'!

In another secondary school, where the staffroom atmosphere was quite different, race issues were never far from the surface amongst the students. At this school there were two Black teachers. The first one, an Afro-Caribbean woman, lasted only one year, because she could not take any more racial abuse from students. The second, a young Asian woman who had grown up in Birmingham, stuck it out. Although she rarely let it show in front of staff or students, she was often worn down by the atmosphere of abuse and hostility. In this kind of situation it is ofter hard for Black teachers to get support from the school because it is easier for the school to explain it as the teacher having a discipline problem rather than the school having a racism problem. Clearly the issues that are raised in this chapter are ones to which there are no comfortable solutions.

In this chapter, the girls discuss the need for Black teachers and reflect on the experience of Black teachers in their schools. They consider whether Black teachers have to compromise their identities in order to succeed and whether Black teachers have certain advantages over white colleagues in experience and understanding. Satnam was one of the participants in our discussion.

Satnam

Satnam's parents are from India. They came to Britain in the 1960s with two young children and settled in London. Satnam and her brother were born in Slough.

The family are now settled in Birmingham where Satnam lives with her parents and brother. Her two older sisters have both married and left home and she is the youngest in the family. Satnam describes her family, who are Sikhs, as quite close. She has a good relationship with her mother; she says: 'I can talk to my mum. I think I'm quite close to her. She's always talking to me, sharing her problems and chatting.'

Satnam considers herself to have quite a lot of freedom, relative to her older sisters. If she wants to go out anywhere during the day she is free to do so as long as her mother knows where she is going and at what time she is expected back.

Her ambition is to work as a nursery nurse in a primary school. She thinks it is very important that when Asian children start school they have people there who can communicate with them in their home language, and remembers how strange she felt when she first started school.

'In the primary school I was at there were very few Asians and all the teachers were white. I felt left out. It would be a good idea to have more Black and Asian teachers. It would help to give the very little children more confidence when they start school.'

Satnam's family give her support in what she wants to do: 'My dad's really pleased. He says I'd better do it in the end. I'd better not just be saying it.'

Satnam expects to have an arranged marriage when she is about twenty. She has some reservations about this as her sister, who had an arranged marriage, is in the process of getting divorced, but she recognizes that love marriages do not always work out either. Her religion means quite a lot to her and she feels it is important to marry someone of the same background.

Satnam feels strongly about the way in which news about India and information about Sikh people is presented in the media. She believes that news coverage of Sikh affairs leaves most British people very ill-informed about important world events and with negative images of India.

Free expression

Tara
'It's very important to have Asian and Black teachers around. Children would feel happier; more confident. They'd know they could ask for anything.'

Cynthia
'You can talk more freely can't you? If it's a white teacher, there tends to be a bit of embarrassment. People may not be able to express themselves so well.'

Elaine
'We were discussing South Africa and intolerance. All the time I could feel the teacher looking at me because he knew I was

interested, and because the rest of the class kept moaning, saying, "This is boring". It was a mainly white class. So he asked, "Who is offended by racist jokes?" Only me and Debbie put our hands up. And they they were all supporting racist jokes, saying it was stupid to be offended, and telling racist jokes. People were laughing. I think that was bad.'

Marcia

'A Black teacher will have had experience with racial discrimination. They will know what they're talking about – and they'll be able to understand the kids. Also if a white teacher says critical things about the white community you don't know where to put yourself. You can feel more relaxed if there's a Black teacher there.'

Jasbir

'You can't exactly talk about your own religion to a white teacher. If it's an Asian teacher or any Black teacher you can ask them questions and they'll answer. My sister talks a lot to Miss L and she does that because she knows she will understand more because she's a Muslim.'

Abuse

Tara

'When I was in junior school we had an Indian teacher and everyone said she looked like my mum. We all enjoyed having her, but the white children laughed at the way that she talked.'

Cynthia

'Miss D came to our school and they constantly poked fun at her. Believe it or not, one boy sat at the back of the classroom and started to smoke. I couldn't believe it. Just because a Black teacher was teaching. They made a joke out of her, and hardly did any work. She was good at her job and when she demonstrated an experiment people started to get really interested. But because of who she was people would use any excuse to give her trouble. Black teachers can carry respect but it takes a lot more. They need to be very strong to show some fools it doesn't matter what colour you are, that you can get somewhere.'

Gillian

'It's not just teachers. I think that all Black people have got to be stronger. We've got to survive.'

Jasbir

'Miss L is very strict. She tells people, "You've got to do this!" and it's done. She still comes back and carries on, even once when the abuse was so bad she ran out of the class.'

Cynthia

'They've made her cry. It's really upsetting. Sometimes she can shout – I don't like her that much personally, but she's all right. I admire her for what she does. She comes in and they've written things about her on the desk, calling her a Paki. I've seen her cry, and run out of the class. She's got courage. She's strong. I don't think I could deal with all that.'

Gillian

'I'd stick it out. That's the sort of person I want to be. That's the sort of thing I want to do. If I have to I'll be the one Black in fifty!'

Elaine

'It should be fairer. It's not right to have all white teachers. We've got a real mixture of kids – white, Black, Greek, Asian, and only white teachers. That's pathetic. I would feel horrible, I mean, only one Asian teacher. Can you imagine, on her own in the staff room? She's got great courage to stay. Others have left, but she's fighting.'

The girls went on to discuss if there were more Black students in the school whether this would prevent Black teachers being abused and driven away. In another school where the majority of the pupils were Black this seemed to be the case:

Erica
'They wouldn't say anything to a Black teacher because if there are Black kids walking past they would look at them and say, "After school". They would only need to look and the white kids would be embarrassed and say, "I didn't mean it in that way."'

Acting white?

Black people remain poorly represented within the teaching profession. Angela's school employs a number of Asian and Afro-Caribbean teachers, one or two of them in senior positions. The girls in this school had mixed feelings about some of these people because they felt they were compromising themselves in order to get on with colleagues.

Angela
'Some Black teachers act white. They're trying to make a good impression on white people and so they act a bit like them, for example, imitate the way they talk. Everything about them – the way they behave, their reactions – is so as to be accepted by white people.'

Pauline
'People with high jobs, they go on like white people. They stick to their rules and their behaviour doesn't suit them at all. They

don't always know they're doing it. They're coconuts, Black on the outside, white on the inside.'

Erica
'Sometimes they know it. They do it because they want to keep their jobs. White people might not like it if they behave like themselves. I'm sorry to say that if it was me, if I was the teacher, I wouldn't compromise. But when they're angry you discover they were pretending. Their behaviour changes and out they come with their Patois. I've heard a teacher say of one, "He should be himself!" and I think that's right.'

Arina
'Even so, there's very few Black teachers around. How many Black headteachers can you think of? When a Black man became head of a big secondary school it was big news in the *Evening Mail*. It was news because it hadn't happened before. Black teachers don't get promoted very easily. One reason there are so few is that they don't want to be stuck at the bottom doing the same thing.'

Asian teachers: 'Only for the Asians!'

Afia
'Ideally there should be equal numbers of Black and white teachers but here we get the white girls saying, "Look they're only for the Asians, we don't want them." They get this kind of rubbish stuck in their minds.'

Nazrah
'Mrs A wears a sari and she teaches the girls who are at an elementary stage in learning English. So white girls think she's not a real teacher. It's doubly hard for her to get respect because people think that she only teaches silly Asian girls and

she's not dressed like a teacher should be. They think she really shouldn't be here anyway, because the Asian girls shouldn't be here.'

Rasheeda
'I think we are less likely to find good Black teachers in secondary school because of the racism that you have to face, there's such a lot of it. Good teachers, like most people, want to be happy in their jobs, rely on their colleagues, and trust the people around them. I don't think that Black people can find that easily in secondary schools. I think they tend to teach in primary school, where they have better control over the children.'

Mumtaz
'I think we don't have many Black teachers in this school because they're probably scared of having racist remarks thrown at them. If we did have them it would be good because all the Black girls would think, "Ah, she's done it or he's done it, that means I can do it too."'

Afia
'White people generally look on us as outcasts. They don't want to get involved in anything we do. Most white teachers live away from us, from Blacks and Asians, so they don't really want to know us. Some people think we shouldn't even be living here, so why get to know us? This negative attitude must be affecting the way many of our white teachers see us. How then can they really know their students?'

What do teachers know?

Cynthia
'It would make you feel better about learning if they acknowledge what you know already. The First Years spent a

whole term studying Jamaica and they did it in geography, English, P.E., and cookery. They learnt Jamaican songs and poetry; they were shown how to cook Jamaican food; and they did Jamaican dancing. Then we had an African teacher who taught us African dancing and told us about songs and about where he was from. He explained the dance is like telling a story, and everyone enjoyed it as well. I thought I'd be good at that, but I wasn't, but it didn't matter.'

Elaine
'It really depends on the individual teacher. If they are interested in something they can find out, or get someone in to help them. Some teachers can't be bothered to find out about other parts of the world or even about Black people here.'

3:
City life

■■

When people ask you where you are from, how do you answer? If you reply something like 'London' or 'Birmingham' or 'Manchester' do they then ask, 'But where are you really from? Where do you originate?' Many Black British people are likely to have this kind of experience when they meet new people or go to a new place.

How do you feel about the place where you live? I asked the girls what they felt about Birmingham. Is it a good place to live? What are the problems living there? What changes would they like to see? Nazrah, Anita and Pauline were amongst those who gave their views.

Nazrah

Nazrah is a lively person who is keen on sport, particularly hockey and netball, and has played a number of times for her school. She likes reading – when we met she was into Horror – and music, 'heavy metal at the moment'. Nazrah also enjoys watching Indian films, particularly comedy, but explained that her parents had recently stopped hiring these videos which they say are no longer family films.

Nazrah was sent to a Jewish primary school where her parents believed she would receive a traditional education. They believed that since Jewish teachers would be offering Jewish children the best then Nazrah would get a first-rate education. As Muslims, her parents would not have to worry about their young daughter being given pork to eat. However, Nazrah felt an outsider and was not very happy there, particularly since most of the children seemed to come from wealthier homes than hers.

Nazrah's father first came to Britain in the mid 1960s as a student. He then went back to Pakistan, married Nazrah's mother and brought her here. At first he worked as a telephone engineer; then the family bought a shop in Small Heath. Her father has been saving so the family can return to Pakistan.

When I met Nazrah all the arrangements had been made to move to Pakistan and the furniture had already been shipped over. She was looking forward to a new life there and her father was looking forward to joining his brothers. Her mother had some reservations, as Nazrah explained: 'My mum's changed a lot since she came here. She's become more modern in her outlook and she's not looking forward to Pakistan because of the in-laws.'

Nazrah expects her new life in Pakistan to be difficult at first. She thinks that she will be a bit behind at school and will have to work hard to catch up. Nazrah has spent holidays in Pakistan and knows that expectations of her there will be different. In our discussions she reflects on Birmingham and on her neighbourhood of Small Heath where she has spent all of her life and which she knows she will miss.

Nazrah knows that in some ways her freedom will be more restricted in Pakistan, for example in the town, or at the single-sex college she will be attending, but she believes that on a day-to-day basis in her family's village she will have more freedom:

'Here girls are packed into their houses. Everyone lives indoors because of the weather. Girls can't go out because of the dangers on the street – being attacked, mugged or raped. But over there, in the village, there are no strangers. You know everybody and you've got your relatives everywhere.'

Anita

Anita was born in Edgbaston, which is where she still lives. Her parents are from Gujerat in India. Her father came to England to study law in the late fifties and Anita's mother joined him in 1962. Her father is a civil servant and her mother works at Austin Rover. Their three children were all born here; Anita is the youngest of three daughters. The family are Hindus.

Anita's parents encourage her in her ambition to study law at university. Her interests tend to be solitary ones; she enjoys reading and listening to music:

'I read a lot, ever such a lot. I read anything, particularly classics. I may read as many as two good books – not rubbish Mills and Boon – a day. And I enjoy listening to music – anything from punk to heavy metal to classical; anything at all, except for opera.'

Anita's father has accused her of rejecting her culture:

'I just had to put him right on that. It's their culture and it's partly mine as well. I can't say it's totally mine, that I'm totally Indian in the way I think. By law I'm British, but I am half Indian and half English really.'

Anita feels very strongly about Asian girls being misrepresented in the media:

'Asian girls in the newspapers are stereotyped as being the ones who have to obey their parents, to stay at home and learn to cook and get married afterwards – that's how Asian girls are seen in the media generally.'

Anita pointed out that while many Asian girls have very limited
freedom, this is not true of all, and that many parents want their
daughters to do well in their education and their careers. She
is also prepared, if necessary, to challenge her own parents'
views.

'I would probably do something behind my mum and dad's
backs if it were something minor. I wouldn't openly defy my
father over something little. But if it were something continual
I'd argue. I would be prepared to see both sides of the
argument but I'd put forward my own views. If I'm given a
good reason for not doing something then I'm prepared to
compromise.'

Pauline

Pauline was brought up in Handsworth and now lives in
Edgbaston. Her mother is from St Kitts and her father from
Jamaica. Pauline and her parents are Rastafarians.
Pauline is well aware that many people hold a number of
misconceptions about Rastafarians and she spent quite a lot of
time trying to explain her way of life and what her religion means
to her:

'It's more important to me than to my parents really. I like
being a Rastafarian. People might wonder why, but I just do.
My religion involves a lot of studying. You have a bible and
you read your bible often. We do things together; we help each
other. It's like the Indian community really, because we have
big get-togethers: everyone comes round; uncles, aunts and
friends.'

She describes her upbringing as very strict:

'They allow me to go out sometimes but not as much as when I was younger . . . I don't mind that. When you get older you get into more trouble. There was supposed to be something on at the Muhammed Ali Centre which I wanted to go to with my cousin. My dad said I could go with her but she was going to London. He wouldn't let me go to the Muhammed Ali Centre on my own, and I wouldn't go on my own.'

Pauline has thought a great deal about the position of Black people in Birmingham and in British society generally and she has strong views on many issues. She is also clear about what she wants to do when she leaves school: 'My grandmother was a midwife in Jamaica and right from when I was little I've always wanted to be a nurse or a doctor.'

Trashy and segregated, but it's home!

Nazrah

'I think Birmingham from the outside view, and from my view, is really dead and really trashy. You look around and there's rubbish everywhere, and I think it's segregated as well. Because if you look at Stirchley and Kings Norton and more up that way, Asians and Blacks get less and less. And if you go up to Selly Oak it's mostly Asians and Blacks everywhere up to Handsworth. And Solihull, again, gets all whites.

'People think that the area you live in reflects the class that you are. When we say to someone that we live in Small Heath they say: "That's a really bad area; don't you want to get out?" Yes, we do want to get out, but we love that area because it is our home. We can't go out because there's loads of gangs there, but still, we've sort of grown to like it more and more. I don't think my dad has or my mum, but us kids have. We've grown to like it and we've made some really good friends without our parents really coming into it. Because most of the people we

know it's through our parents. But in Small Heath whichever
shop we go into we make friends with them.'

Best place to be!

Anita

'I like Birmingham. I don't think there's any other sort of town
I'd really like to live in. I just like Birmingham, it's good. Most of
the people are kind of friendly and open; I mean it's a good sort of
mix in Birmingham. I must admit there are some areas which are
heavily populated with Indians or white people or whatever.'

Whites only

Afia

'If an Asian or a Black goes into an area like Solihull or Kings
Norton you feel weird. You feel you're in the wrong place.
Solihull is conservative and they're all whites. I know an Asian
family in there and they find it quite difficult, but then again
they say to themselves that they've adapted to Solihull – but I
went there and felt really different. Everyone was looking at us
and thinking "God, she's an Asian" and I thought, "What am I
doing here?"'

Mumtaz

'I think if you're Black or Asian and you go to live in rich or
white areas you change the whole of your lifestyle. You have to
be posh and show you're really educated. People think that
because you live in the inner city you're bound to be stupid.
Because we're Asians as well they put more down on us. If I
went to live in a posh area I'd feel uncomfortable but I
wouldn't develop right into their ways. I'd keep my own
culture, my own way of living.'

Rasheeda

'I quite like where I live (Moseley) and I've got all sorts of Asian friends, not many whites though. I wouldn't feel comfortable if we were the only persons living there, surrounded by whites. You'd be picked on. Around people would be saying, "Oh, look at them, let's start playing them up" and things like that. I quite like it where I am. I prefer it mixed so that there's equal Blacks and equal whites living in a particular area.'

No-go areas?

Satnam

'My dad wanted to buy a shop in Great Barr because it was going cheap. It was all dirty and my mum didn't like it and was against the idea, but my dad kept on trying to persuade us so we moved. We had to start by cleaning and tidying the place up. Nobody really made us welcome round that area, because there's mostly whites round there and we were the only Indian family.

'The shop was beginning to go really well and then one night our window got smashed; somebody broke it with a brick. We had the police in. My mum kept saying: "I told you we shouldn't have moved here". There was a lot of racism so we moved back to our old house.'

Marcia

'My cousin has had a similar experience to Satnam's family. He's just gone into business and moved up Kingstanding way. He says people have come round and threatened him but they haven't actually broken any windows or anything. He's on the main road, on the 33 bus route and he's had a lot of racist remarks. There's another Black man who runs a business further up the road and he's had trouble; he's got serious with them and got into trouble with them.'

Cynthia
'On our road there are houses going up for sale. An Indian family wanted to move into one. There are quite a lot of white people in the road and only three Black families. The family did the house up ready to live in but my dad was talking to the Indian guy and he was thinking of letting it because his wife didn't think it was suitable. She talks to my mum and she says she doesn't really want to live there because everyone else is looking at her; my mum is the only one talking and it seems as if people don't want her up the road.'

Gillian
'On my estate when we first moved in there were only two Black families and now there are two more Indian families, and one Black family who have just moved in. It's only in the past year that I've been feeling all right in the area. Before you used to have people saying things and writing on the pavement or whatever. They don't do it any more.'

Elaine
'My mum's white and my dad's Black. Yesterday I went with my sister and mum to Lichfield. It's somewhere where we used to go together when we were little, but probably I didn't know about these things then. We were in this massive park. I only saw about two other Black kids in the whole of this great park and I didn't like it. I was waiting for someone to say something. There were these three girls watching us all the time and I was just waiting for them to say something. It wouldn't have been the first time it's happened. That was Lichfield and I hardly saw anyone Black there. I just didn't feel right in that park.'

Handsworth: riot or rebellion?

The girls were eager to discuss the Handsworth riots, which took place in September 1985. Like many Birmingham people, they felt angry about the way in which some newspapers reported on events, focusing on the part played by Black people and on divisions in the Black community, particularly between Asian and Afro-Caribbean people. This was clearly seen to be a distortion of the truth. The girls recognized that these media reports had affected the way many outsiders view Birmingham, and also how many Birmingham people view Handsworth. Talking some eighteen months after the events, the girls explained what they thought had happened and why.

Anita
'I live right on the Ladywood–Edgbaston border. I think the cause of the bad reputation was the riots and what people read about them. Now when anybody talks about Birmingham or Handsworth they usually speak of the riots straightaway.'

Gillian
'Tension built up because of certain problems. It was one thing after another which caused the Black people, the Asian people and also the white people of Handsworth to rebel. They decided they couldn't take it any more. So they decided to rebel in a way that everyone would notice.'

Marcia
'I've noticed living in Handsworth that they've got loads of publicity. It was on the news a couple of months ago that more jobs have been made. That's what started the riots. There weren't many jobs for the Black people around the area. They were all out of jobs and on the dole. When you go up to the dole office you see a long queue of whites, Blacks and Asians.

'What started it going was a Black who was offended by a white policeman. The police threw him against the side of the bus and he broke his leg. Some of these Black and Asian guys who were up that end by Villa Cross saw it and got really offended by it and started arguing. Then more cops came down and started a havoc, and the buses were stopped and everything. Then about an hour later it must have all started, and shops were burned down, and there were loads of people coming down: Blacks, whites and Asians. But it was the Black people of Handsworth that was blamed.

'I was looking out of my window and I saw Blacks, whites and Asians. You name it, people running up and down my road, they were all sorts. I really thought it was bad to put in the paper or on the news, you know: "Black and Asian people of Handsworth". In the paper one or two white people were listed down and the majority were Black.

'It was because of the jobs. In a way they've been successful because they've got more jobs. Handsworth itself has been looked at, and they've realized it was a bad area for jobs. In a way they've failed because a lot of people have gone to prison for it.'

Photos can lie

Pauline
'It was as much Indians and white people in Handsworth as Black, and it wasn't just the Rastafarians; of course, it was all of them really, everybody was putting their bit into it.

'Handsworth is an area you can't really say you're going to put a law on to it. It's an area where everybody likes to live and just go as they are. Teenagers, everybody, grows up in Handsworth; if a new person comes to Handsworth they're spotted straightaway. I used to live just off the Lozells Road so had we been there we would have been close to the riot. People would probably have thought, well my family would've went right in and got in with the riot as well. But some Black people wasn't even there. If you was to look back they took photographs of the Black people, but if you was to take a photograph of everybody you'd see as many white faces and Indian faces as there was Black faces there.'

YTS: a solution?

Mumtaz
'I think the government invented YTS to get the youths off the streets, so that when they leave school they have somewhere to go if they don't want to carry on with their education. They thought that by providing a pay packet that young people would be interested in it. They haven't put a lot of thought into the scheme; they haven't worked out the training aspect. They are just trying to cut down on disturbances. I wouldn't go on one because I don't like wasting my time. I like to get to the point of things.'

Rasheeda
'I think with YTS the employers mainly want white people and the schemes can't operate fairly because they depend on the employers.'

Afia
'I think they are trying to figure out a way of getting rid of unemployment. I wouldn't go because "Youth Training Scheme" is a contradiction in terms. You don't get much training. They've got to make it good for the youths, not promise a girl secretarial training and then let her run around making coffee and tea. Once you've completed your "training" and you want to carry on the employers say "no". The government talk in clichés, they don't do anything.'

Who cares?

Elaine

'I don't live in Handsworth. I just hear from the news. Some of the young kids were running against the government and trying to get them to listen to them. I think that when Prince Charles came down everybody tried to understand why and tried to be really sympathetic. And now everybody seems to forget about it again. Nobody seems to be bothered.'

Cynthia

'It may be to do with the way people live. The flats might get them down, especially when you're unemployed and young. They might think, "Oh God, is this all I've got, this council house?" People waiting ages to get something fixed, and then it's not done properly. All right, jobs was one of the causes, but another cause was the police. When they drive past they look slow and watch when you're walking down the road. They look at all the Blacks and the Asians; you know people feel sort of offended. I've heard Blacks and Asians saying how much they hate the police. And you know that's why when the policeman hurt the Black guy, that's why it started. So it is jobs and it is also because they just don't get on with the police.'

Divided community?

Anita

'In this newspaper report about what caused it there was some rubbish about noisy parties. I don't think it was any of that. I think it was police harassment, and there's racism and, well, unemployment. The police have some good ideas but they just go about them in the wrong way. I guess the police – I can't really judge them because individually some of them are right horrible people and some police I guess must be all right. I can't speak.

'Between Black and Asian people, between some it's a problem how they get on. Like, if an Afro-Caribbean person went into an Asian person's shop some Asian shopkeepers keep a special eye on them. Yet if an Indian person went in they'd be all right. It depends on the individual really because there's not many problems between them. The newspapers do seem to exaggerate a lot of stuff and particularly if a paper is biased they'll put whatever they write just to back their own sort of opinion.'

Brothers and sisters

Pauline

'Black people have a lot that they share with Indian people. I know a white lady and when an Indian taxi came she turned round and said she never ordered the taxi because she seen it was an Indian person in the cab and she goes "Oh no, I didn't want that, I didn't order a taxi" and then she went to order a different one. She went and phoned TOA Taxis because they're mainly white people there. But if my dad phones for a taxi if the car's broken down, if my dad goes into a cab with an Indian person I'm surprised because sometimes I'm sitting in the back of the car and they're talking as if they've known each other for years and years and they've probably just met each other. Some Black people treat Indian people like their brothers and sisters.'

Black police

Rasheeda

'After the Handsworth riots the police on TV tried to change their image by saying that they wanted to recruit more Black and Asian policemen. That was only after the riots; they didn't say anything before. Because after the riots they thought the whole country was looking at them and thinking it's full of white policemen and, you know, they're all racist. And so they're trying to improve the situation, but I think they knew that Blacks and Asians don't really want to be in the police force because if they did their own people would think they were being traitors. And so, if you look now there are still many more white policemen, and if you look at the sergeants and the more senior officers – the people at the head – there are even fewer Blacks. I think there's not one in ten who even becomes a sergeant who's Black.

Rasheeda

'I think there should be equal Black and white in the police force, but if there were Blacks the white police might often go against them and not treat them properly. Even if Black people pass a special exam to join the police force that's really not worth it because the white police are always going to treat the Black police as not, you know, part of the police force, I think.'

Mumtaz

'I think the police force should be mixed but it will be difficult because it's hard for the Blacks and Asians to go to the police force because it's a new thing and they haven't experienced it before. They don't know what's going to happen and what reactions they're going to get from both the people around them and from the police force.'

Token Blacks

Afia

'It may be a problem, for example, if a white family have trouble and a Black policeman came to sort it out. They might think "What's he doing here? He's right for racism, for an issue between Black and white, or for dealing with Black people. I don't want him, I want the white police. I can explain myself better." They might use Black people only to sort Black people out – just to keep them employed for one thing, thinking that's all they're good for. Just have the whites for all the important bits.'

Avoiding the police

Nazrah

'Last week some friends of ours had some bother and she didn't want to phone the police; she asked my dad to, because my dad's got sort of a snobby accent. My dad phoned the solicitor, but whenever the police come, whenever it's an Asian person, the police really take their time and when they do come there's tons and tons of them. But when it's whites the police come, sort of quicker, but there's less of them.

'Punks and Asians had some trouble in front of our house not very long ago and the police arrived and they took mostly Asians in, Asians and Blacks. A few whites got taken in. And this Asian guy got his head battered in with glass by another gang and nothing happened to them. Just the person who got hit was taken in by the police.'

Afia

'If it was a big problem, then we'd have to turn to the police you know. We'd have to. But, like, if it was a little problem we'd try to avoid the police; just solve it if we can. I think if someone phones and they're Asian, if you can tell by the way they talk that they're Asian, then the police act differently. They talk extra slow and really exaggerate.'

Uniting against racism

Nazrah
'I think Asians and Blacks should support each other but they're different sorts of people and they experience different racism. But if they do get together I think it would be easier because they experience similar racism too. I think that Blacks and Asians should stick together because they both really are outsiders in England.'

Afia
'I think that where possible Blacks, Asians and whites should stick together to sort out these problems of racism.'

Blacks MPs : cause for hope?

Mumtaz
'I think that in those areas of the country where Black MPs were elected it might make a difference to Black people. But in the rest of the country they just think "Oh, four, that's nothing" and just ignore them. But I think to make a difference you've got to have many more.'

Rasheeda
'I think that being a Black MP in the House of Commons will be like being a Black teacher in this school. They're going to find it tough. If a Black person wants to speak out they may be put down.'

Marcia
'Those Black MPs, they give us all courage.'

Afia

'When politicians say, "There isn't any racism in my party" they are just being stupid because of course racism exists. They are just not facing up to the reality of the world. How can their party be outside of that reality? So if the Labour Party say, "Look, we're not racist, we've got MPs" they must also think about what they are doing for the MPs and for the Black and Asian community.

'Politicians say that everything is going to be all right, but nothing is going to be all right now. Everything is just going to get worse now that the big Mrs T's still in. She didn't do anything worthwhile for the last four years. I'm just waiting to see what she's going to do now and then let the people decide.'

Mumtaz

'In Pakistani culture your name, your respect, is most important. Most of these Asian councillors they are doing it for the name. The Conservative politicians in our area relied on the Asians in the community to vote for them. They hoped that people would think, "Oh, he's an Asian, he's bound to do good for us." When they went around doing their electioneering they relied on the Asian people. But I think that some Asian people have definitely got more sense and didn't vote for them, because they haven't been elected.'

Nazrah

'If they are going to be successful politicians they've got to represent everyone in the area. It's not just Asians living there, there are English too, and some are more badly off than the Asians there.'

Afia

'I think that the people of London and other places may think of Birmingham as a place of riots. They may imagine Black and

Asian youths rioting all the time and just destroying the city. They have a low opinion of Birmingham; much lower than of London. But it is getting better and people are trying to sort out the problems of racism here.'

Cynthia
'It doesn't matter what race you are – it shouldn't matter.'

Gillian
'I'd like to live somewhere where it's mixed, where you don't have to worry about your colour, where you can go about doing what you want, being what you want to be, not being looked upon as Black or white.'

4:
Friends and
boyfriends

■■■

What attracts us to our friends is sometimes difficult to explain, and it certainly would be boring if all our friends were alike. Talking with close friends can be a way of finding out more about ourselves.

Boys are another puzzle. Do real-life boys match up to the romantic images? Is it possible to have straightforward friendships with boys, and how do parents react to this? How does having a boyfriend affect friendships and family?

Erica

Erica lives with her mother in Small Heath. Her mother came to Britain with her own parents as a small baby in 1957. Her grandparents were from Jamaica and they first emigrated to America but stayed only a few months before moving again and settling in Britain.

Erica's father is also from Jamaica. He came to live here in 1967 when he was ten years old. Erica's parents separated when she was a baby:

'There's just me and my mum and the dog at home. We've been together for ages because my mum left my dad before I was one. We went to live with my grandad, my mum's dad. Then we moved into our own flat and we went on from there. I see my dad sometimes, but not that often.'

Erica's mother works in an office and Erica's ambition is to get a well-paid job, possibly as an accountant, which will support them both:

'I don't want to stay over here; I'd like to go to America. My mum says I've got to get all my qualifications first. She says I ain't going nowhere until I've had a proper education. I want to do something where I can earn good money to keep the both of us. My mum says she's fed up of keeping us now. It's my turn to look after both of us.'

Erica sees a lot of her family, many of whom live close by. She also has family in London and in America, which is one of the reasons she's attracted to living there. She enjoys swimming and other sports, and likes going out with her friends occasionally to nightclubs. She thinks her mum gives her enough freedom to do most of what she wants to do:

'It's enough for me. Some parents give their kids more freedom but I'm all right. At the moment she won't let me pierce my ears again, which is stupid. If I go out, it depends on who I'm going with. If she knows and trusts the person I'm going out with that's fine, but otherwise she'll say no, "Because I don't really know who you're getting in with and what you're doing."'

'She's all right with boyfriends, if I decide to tell. I don't always tell her. First of all she gives me a lecture: "You know what you should do, you know what you shouldn't do" and everything, but that's it. If they come to the house she's not like some mums, "I don't want him sitting here: I don't want him in here!" She's all right.

'I'd prefer to be out with my friends than with a boy. I'd go to the picture house with a boy or he can take me to McDonalds, but I wouldn't go out with him at night. I don't think it's me to go out on my own with a boy. Maybe in a couple of years, but I don't feel mature enough to be out with boys. The one I'm going out with now is eighteen, that's not much older than these ones at school. But at his age they are much more mature.'

Arina

Arina was born in Birmingham and lives in Handsworth. Her father came to Britain from Trinidad in 1959; his family are of Asian descent. Arina's mother came to Britain in 1964, leaving her own parents behind in Bangladesh. Arina's parents have separated, and Arina lives with her mother, her stepfather and her younger brothers and sisters. Arina's natural father died recently, but she has always looked upon her stepfather as her dad, as he has brought her up. He is also from Bangladesh and the family are Muslims.

Arina's parents are both unemployed, although her mother takes in some sewing from time to time. Her stepfather used to work as a maintenance engineer in a factory, but has been out of work for many years.

The family are talking about emigrating and Arina's mother would like to go back to Bangladesh to her own mother as she fears she may never see her again. Arina's mother has talked about taking Arina to America to stay with relations there because she cannot persuade her to go to Bangladesh with the rest of the family. Arina is very keen to travel; she finds home life a bit claustrophobic with two younger brothers and a little sister.

Arina's mother has given her quite a lot of freedom, but she is trying to bring up her younger children in a more religious way:

'Religion is quite an important thing in my family. My dad tries to go to the mosque every night and he always goes on Fridays. My mum is not that religious but she does read the Koran at home and she does the prayers. My dad does all the prayers and my mum does them when she's got time. They made us learn Arabic, so we would know how to read the

Koran, but they left it a bit late with me, I'm past all that now. They are stricter with the little ones because they don't want them to turn out like us. I don't feel strongly about religion, but I think it's important that I know a little about it and about my culture, my background.'

Arina likes going out to parties and occasionally to nightclubs, when she can persuade them she's old enough to get in. She spends a lot of time listening to music and reads lots of magazines.

At school . . .

Jasbir
'It wasn't that hard to make friends when I changed schools because everyone was quite friendly in the class. They weren't picking on new people, saying her hair is like that or that she looks like that. No one was like that to me, so that was a good start to the year anyway. It wasn't that bad but I did find it hard to settle because I really wanted to stay at my old school.'

Elaine
'I hated it when I first arrived. I sometimes felt like killing myself because I had no friends at all. The very first time I came I was late and Sarah made friends with me. I've hung around with most of the girls in my class. In the third year I got to know Marcia and the rest of them.

'You have got to give and take in relationships with friends. There are some days you come to school and you're in a mood and some days when you're really happy. I think we're all sort of loyal to each other. Say someone goes on about my friend's religion, I may not like it that much but I'll stick up for her.'

Angela
'I didn't really settle until the second year because I found it hard to make friends when I arrived. I was the only one from

my junior school and they used to all laugh at me and make my life a misery.'

Erica
'It was hard to make friends with people outside your class because they were demanding stuff off you, saying it was their birthday or demanding money off you.'

Marcia
'When I started in the first year I felt a bit left out because my name was strange and I hated it. The teachers used to pronounce it wrongly and I just hated it. Another thing was that I was travelling a distance because I didn't want to go to a school around my area. I wanted to make new friends. I knew a few people in this area as well as in Handsworth, so I came to this school. I've made loads of friends and the first person I met I got on with.'

Secrets

Satnam
'You have to trust a friend if you tell them something. It's not nice if you tell someone a secret and the next day you come to school and lots of other people have been told by her. Then you don't want to know her anymore. You discover that some friends you have are like that. Some friends you can trust and tell them everything and you know they won't tell anybody. With some you know they'll tell anybody, so you just have to make sure you've got the right friends.'

Afia
'You wouldn't really want to develop a friendship with someone who will take advantage of you, saying to themselves that you are kind and they will be able to get anything off you.

I don't like people who use you. You've got to have trust and loyalty in a relationship. You may have a fight sometimes, that's perfectly normal, but I don't like the kind who just use you and then turn out to be really two-faced, talking behind your back.'

Careful choice

Afia
'When you're choosing friends first of all you notice the people who are loud and then you begin to see what people are really like, whether someone is kind, whether they have the same interests as you. From then you make friends with people that have something in common with you.'

Gillian
'When I first came I was really loud and I used to go around with everyone. Now I've got many friends. A friend has got to be a laugh but then again, she's got to be loyal. She's got to respect me for what I am and me her.'

Anita
'I've made most of my friends through lessons. You start off talking about what you've been doing in school and you make friends from there. But I don't see many of them after school because not many of them live near me. My friends are quite a mixture. They're not all Asian and they're not all Black, but there aren't a lot of white girls in my part of our year group.'

Tara
'I didn't find it difficult to make friends because my cousin came to the school at the same time. We were both in the same class. Out of school I tend to spend some of my time with my cousins.'

Afia

'If you are of the same religion it helps because you know what the other is talking about, but I don't really think that's the most important thing. As far as I'm concerned I don't care what a person's background is as long as the person themselves is all right. The important thing is the person inside, that's what I'm looking at.'

Erica

'I like people who can think for themselves, not those who are always agreeing with you.'

Mumtaz

'I think I've selected my friends just by talking to them, and by watching them as well to get to know them. You get to know most people and then from that point you choose which ones you prefer. My close friends are Asian and I don't think I'm really close to any white girls. You know them, you say "hello", but you don't really get on any deeper level. I think it's better to have friends from the same background because you understand each other and you trust each other more. There's no special reason why I wouldn't trust white girls, it's just that they live a different life from us. We're like two different kinds of people.'

Erica

'It's easier to make friends with white people than with Black people because Black people are fussy when it comes to friends. White people seem to hang around with anybody. I'd rather hang around with Black people because I'm Black and I feel more comfortable with Black people than with white. The way white people carry on don't suit me at all.'

White friends

Nazrah

'I go for someone with a good sense of humour and the same interests as me. I mostly get on with Asians but in our class there's one white girl who I used to be really close with in the second year. We got to know each other because at one point all the class got a good yelling at and we were made to sit with people that we didn't know. I was put next to an English girl and we really got on well and had right laughs together. We would go around together, but then other white girls would be there and we started hanging around with them. They used to talk about "What boy are you going out with?" and "Shall we go down to the park tonight?" I couldn't really come in with the conversation like this and so we just gradually drifted apart. It's a bit of a shame really because we could have made really good friends. We still talk to each other and so on, but she mainly sticks to them because she doesn't really want to know what's going on with me now.'

Satnam

'If you've got an Asian friend I think it's easier. You can talk more freely and tell them what's happened at home. You can talk in your own language. But if you've got a white friend you can't really talk. You might feel a bit shaky. You can't really say what you feel. Somebody who's Black will probably understand what I'm saying because we'll have something in common, even if we are from different cultures, but someone who's white probably won't even know what I'm going on about.'

Arina

'I don't really know any white girls. I say hello to them but that's about it. It's just the way that it started and that's how it's really worked out. They probably like to go to different places. I enjoy going to parties, dancing, the carnival and the Handsworth Festival.'

Tara
'I don't hang around much with white girls. I think you can share more with Black and Asian girls. I think I just get on better with them.'

Angela
'I've got one white friend that I still go out with but she used to be into my kind of music, soul and funk, and she used to go to all the dances with us but now she doesn't. We still talk and tell each other quite a lot.'

Best friends

Gillian
'My best friend is my cousin. She's someone I can fall back on and someone I can really trust. She's got to be like my mother really, always there.'

Angela
'I don't deal in best friends because you'd get bad feeling, with someone saying that she thought she was your best friend. But I do have close friends that I get on better with, the ones that it's easier to talk to. At school there are friends you hang around with that you wouldn't see after school or arrange to go places with.'

Elaine
'My mum is my best friend I think. I had a best friend but she went horrible. I hang around with some girls and we all get on really well, but they're not my best friends.'

Afia

'The most important time when you want friends to be around is when you've got a problem and you want to confide in a friend. I think to be a friend you've got to have a special quality in just being there and listening. The sorts of things that we usually talk about as friends are boys, or when you're at school, the teachers. But the other thing we want to talk about is what's going on in the world. We'll have a kind of debate between us, talking about politics, saying, "Oh they can't do that! They can't do this!"'

Arina

'I like it when we're all out in a big group or we are doing something that we'll all remember, enjoying ourselves. We've had some really good times we know we'll all remember. I don't like people who are too serious, always arguing about things.'

True love and romance? No thanks!

Afia

'I think you can have a good relationship with a boy, not necessarily as girlfriend and boyfriend, but as good friends. You can really get on with boys, you can find out that you have the same interests. My brother, most of his friends are girls and he really gets on with them. But not as in true love and romance!'

Tara

'I think having girls as friends is important because, if you have a boyfriend, you can't exactly tell him all your problems. But you can tell a girl and you can trust her. Girls know what it's like and you know how they feel as well.'

Marcia

'I don't have a boyfriend right now. I did have one, but to tell the truth I get on better with guys if they're just friends. Now I hang about with three girls and about three guys. They'll call for me and we'll just go to the club, a youth club. There's pool, snooker and table tennis and then there's a hall where you can listen to music one night, and then the next night there's basketball, netball or volleyball. We've had day trips to London, and you can mix around and get to meet people.

'I used to go out with this guy, and now I can tell him things, but when he was my boyfriend I couldn't. He was still fun to be with, but there weren't as many jokes. I thought he'd probably think I was stupid if I had a laugh, and I didn't want him to think that, but we're good friends now.'

No freedom

Jasbir

'With a friend you expect to go out with her, perhaps to parties or perhaps to the cinema. I'd really like to go out, perhaps on a Sunday, or any other day. But at home our mum won't let us out. She won't let us go shopping, to the library, or anywhere. We just can't go. That's the way it is.

'I don't remember going out with a friend anywhere. We've got a real close family, and my mum's brother's children – two girls, two boys – we tell them everything. Me and my sister really get on with them, and of course I have a few close friends at school, so friends are not a problem. It's just that they won't accept us going out of the house. In fact if they saw you somewhere talking to a boy, say at dinner time in the high street, one of our cousins or uncles will start making up stories and it will go straight to our parents. I don't know what they've got against boys. They think girls who talk to boys are bad. They always get the wrong impression.

'I feel really isolated all the time at home. If my friends phone me up then my dad is always going mad. The point is that I can't go to see my friends so I want them to phone. If I get a letter from a friend then my mum is questioning me about the letter: "Who's your friend? What's her name? Where does she live? What does she do?" Always questioning. She knows I hate it.'

Rasheeda

'I haven't got any freedom at all. I can't go anywhere. I just have to stay in the house. So the only chance I have to get out is to say I have to go to the library. And even when I go to the library I have to take my brother with me, so they don't let me go out anywhere. They just expect me to be at home and be hardworking around the house. My brother is sent with me to the library to spy on me in case I do anything wrong.'

Innocent rebels

Afia

'I think that if your parents treat you like Rasheeda's do then that's wrong and you're going to rebel. They think that if she doesn't go anywhere and do anything then she'll stay sweet and innocent. But the girls that do go out, at least they get to know about life, and they get to know what's what and where to go and where not to because it's dangerous. But if they keep you at home and you don't know what's going on outside then you are going to be vulnerable when you do get out. Those girls are not going to stay all innocent; they will rebel and that's when their parents will regret it.'

Rasheeda

'I just long to go out. I'd love to go anywhere. I wouldn't care as long as I'm out of the house. I'm in the house and there are four more who are younger than me. I just have to look after them.'

Running off with boys

Afia

'My mum didn't really mind whether I went to a mixed school, all she was concerned about was that I should get on with my education. "She has to work, I don't mind where she goes but she has to work." It was my dad who made me go to a girls' school. He thinks I'm going to run off with the first boy that I meet, but that's really silly. Even though he's my father he doesn't really know me properly. I'm not the kind of girl who would do that, I wouldn't go out with a boy just for the sake of it, just because it's something that I'm not supposed to do. I just want to get on with my education. If I want to go to town with a friend I always get questioned: "Where are you going? Why do you want to go? What time will you be back? Who's this friend of yours?" I think that's all right but they overdo it a bit. You've got to have a trusting relationship with your parents, if you haven't got that then it's the end.'

Mumtaz

'If I was to talk to a boy I think my mum would question me about who it was and what I was talking about. When I go on to college it will be mixed, because I don't know of any single-sex colleges, and my parents know I will have to get on with people in my class. My sister has to talk to the boys in her class and my mum sees her and doesn't mind because she knows she's not going to fall in love or something silly like that. I find that good that our parents should trust us so I trust them as well.'

Satnam

'My family let me go out, but they don't let me go out alone because I don't think they really trust me. If they saw me talking to a boy there would be trouble. They'd say everybody is going to talk about you now. They'd say your dad wears a turban and you should be loyal to him, not go around doing all these things.'

Nazrah

'I don't think that my mum and dad think I'm going to go after boys. I mean we're not allowed anyway. We're not allowed out, the only excuse we've got to go out is to go to the library. I haven't got any boys as friends because I don't really go out anywhere where I might meet them. The only boy I can count amongst my friends he's really funny. He's a really good laugh.'

Satnam

'My mum and dad don't mind who I mix with as far as girls are concerned. That's to say, they're not racist or anything, they just worry about boys.'

Tara

'For me it's a bit different. There could be trouble but it's generally all right. I wouldn't be worried if my cousin saw me talking to boys. I've a cousin who only lives two doors away and she wouldn't grass on me or anything like that. I wouldn't be worried by whatever my uncles might say because since my parents separated my dad wouldn't take any notice of whatever my mum's brothers might say.'

Gillian

'My dad gets really serious about these things. I was coming out of the club with about six fellas and we were all mucking about because we'd just finished a lesson and were all in a good mood. They were picking me up and throwing me about. They're always doing it. My aunt walked past and gave me a dirty look. I don't get on with my aunt and we have massive arguments, but I said "hello" just to be polite, because I thought she was going to throw a scene and I don't like to be shouted at. She said "hello" and everything and then walked on. The next day she came to my house telling my mum that I was kissing these fellas and that it was more than one. My dad banned me from doing training for about two months. He just didn't listen to me, only to my aunt.

'My dad expects me to get on with my work in school, stop in, do all my housework, the cooking, and that's it. He doesn't really expect me to go out and meet this fella and that fella. Now I don't get so much housework because I've got more commitments at training. Nearly a year I've been training and I think my dad's getting used to it now so he doesn't really moan that much.'

Boy company

Angela
'It's difficult to say that the person you're going out with is more or less important to you than your friends. The person I've got now, I can't compare him to my friends. I just hope I get on with both, and that one doesn't come between me and the other.'

Erica
'It's important that you can share certain sorts of things with a good friend. You should be able to talk about your problems, man trouble for instance. You'd talk that over with your friends but you'd keep it quiet with your parents. My mum sometimes says to me that I'm too young, but if she knows there's a

problem she doesn't interfere, she says she hopes I will sort it out.'

Marcia

'When I was going out with a guy my mum sort of knew but she didn't really say anything because she knew I'd start arguing with her. A boyfriend is really just someone to be with because I don't like to be with girls all the time. At school I'm with the girls but out of school I'm with other people, and perhaps with a boyfriend. My dad doesn't mind, my sisters don't mind, but my brothers think I should watch what I'm doing. I think about what I am doing. My mum might ask me where I'm going, and if I say I'm going down the road she'll say I should be back by a certain time. Sometimes she'll moan and say boys keep coming to the house. But I say, "Mum, you say I should keep boy company as well as girls, so why can't they come to the house to meet me?" She says that she gets on better with man than with woman, because she's got more men friends than women friends, well, so do I. But she sees it differently from the way that I see it. She can have a man friend but she says no to me. Boys used to knock at the door and she used to moan and argue but now that I'm fifteen she's not so harsh about it. She says as long as it's a friend, and if she knows I'm going out with somebody she says as long as I'm careful, that's it.'

Be careful!

Marcia

'She means watch what you're doing. Because one of my older sisters she was eighteen and she got pregnant. My mum thought that was bad. She didn't go mad but she doesn't want to see another one in the family at eighteen or even younger. Around where I live there are lots of girls around fifteen, even younger, third or fourth years, and they've had kids. She just doesn't want that to happen to me.'

Cynthia
'My mum wouldn't say anything to me. She wouldn't exactly ask me if I'm going out with anyone. My dad's not for it at all. My sisters say I mustn't go out with anyone white and I ask them why not. They're just being horrible. I say it's up to me but they think it's not up to me but up to them. They say that a white guy will probably get you into trouble and I say so will a Black guy. They put so many restrictions on who I can go out with so I haven't really been out with anyone that much.'

Erica
'These boys at school are fourteen going on fifteen, or fifteen already. All they can think about is the one thing: sex. Lawfully, they're not old enough to do what they want to do, but they're bragging about it and everything. If you go out with someone older, just two or three years older, they may be old enough to do what they want to do but they won't go on about it. They haven't got it on the brain all the time. They're more mature.'

Arina
'When it comes to boys and all that business I keep it to myself or my friends but I don't tell my mum anything. If a phone call comes and it's a boy then she finds out, but usually I don't tell her anything, because it's got nothing to do with her. Parents get the wrong idea. They think you are going to have sex before your age, jump into bed, and come out pregnant. That's all they think about.'

Erica
'My mum says she doesn't mind boyfriends as long as I'm careful and I know I am so that's OK. The thing is that a

mother is scared before anything has happened. But the girl herself, she probably isn't thinking about doing anything. It's the parents who get the wrong idea. People think that because you've got a boyfriend and because you know about sex that's what you're going to do. If you think the average boyfriend lasts three months, then that's not long enough to decide to sleep with someone. Even if I was old enough, even if I wanted to and he wanted to I wouldn't because that's not long enough for me to decide to sleep with him. Not six months either.'

5:
Our past . . .
and our future

■■■

Clearly it was not some accident which brought the Black community to Britain, yet the history taught in schools often neglects to explain why there are Black people living in this country. Even when the subject is covered, the story is usually told from the perspective of white historians and rarely in the words of the Black people whose story it is.

Many British people know little or nothing about the historical relationship between Britain and the people of the Caribbean and the Indian subcontinent which has developed over hundreds of years. Those who have studied something of this relationship in school often fail to make the links between it and the migration of Black people from these places to Britain which began in the late forties and the early fifties. Certain events are emphasized and some are ignored.

It is very difficult to write history while it is happening but, in a way, this is what the girls in this book are attempting to do by recording their experiences of living in Britain today.

Elaine

Elaine lives with her parents and younger brother in Erdington. Her mother is English and her father is from Jamaica. He came to Britain with his parents when he was eleven years old. When Elaine's parents married they lived first in Handsworth and then in Castle Vale before settling in Erdington.

Elaine says that because her father moved to Britain when he

*was a child he doesn't talk to her much about Jamaica, so she has
set out to find out for herself more about her family's history and
about history and politics generally. She has turned to her
grandparents for some of this information, and the rest she has
sought from books:*

'I've learned about it myself by reading. I know it's a waste of
time waiting for the teachers to say anything about it. I've
found out about slavery and I've also learned about South
Africa. I think we ought to study more about these things:
about apartheid; about the IRA and the situation in Belfast;
because these things affect ordinary people, innocent people
who are really in trouble. We ought to know about the
American civil rights movement. I've had to learn on my own
about Martin Luther King. It's my own background that's
made me more interested in these things.'

*Elaine likes company, and spends most of her spare time chatting
with her friends or with her mother whom she considers to be her
best friend. Elaine describes herself as someone with a tendency to
talk too much. She hopes to go on to college to study drama and art.*

Afia

*Afia's father came to Britain from Pakistan in the mid 1960s to
find work. Her mother, who was a teacher in Pakistan, came here
at about the same time to join her married sister. Her brother-in-
law made the arrangements for her marriage, and so Afia's parents
were married soon after her mother arrived. They are Muslims.*

*Afia's father has had quite a number of permanent jobs with
West Midlands Transport. Her mother has remained a housewife
but wishes she had the experience of working in this country. Afia
says of her mother:*

'She was quite a good teacher, but she came over here and she's forgotten everything. She wishes that before I was born she'd got a job – she's regretting it now because we're a bit short of money.'

Afia lives with her parents and her brother who is seventeen. She finds home life quite stressful because her mother's health is quite poor; she suffers from depression and sometimes gets confused. As a consequence of this, Afia, as the only girl in the family, has quite a lot of responsibilities. Afia's parents do not get along, and their quarrels get her down. Afia is close to her mother but she feels frustrated that both her parents share their problems with her:

'My mother depends on me and if mum and dad start quarrelling my mum always comes to me. She starts blaming it on me and I get really mad. I say, "Why don't you tell my brother? You're always telling me." She says that he doesn't listen but that's not true. She hasn't tried telling him, he would listen.

'Then my dad comes to me and he says, "You're the girl of the house and you should do this and you should do that" and I get really desperate. Sometimes I feel like running away for a bit and then coming back. I just wish that everything was all right.'

Afia expects to do well in her GCSEs and then go on to do her A levels. She wants to go to art college in London, to get some experience in fashion, and then to start her own business. Her father would like her to be an accountant.

Afia includes drawing and art, music magazines, and food – 'but not cooking' – amongst her hobbies. She is well informed about current affairs and concerned about the racism and sexism that

Asian women face. Her other ambition is to travel: 'I should love to see Japan.'

Marcia

Marcia is the youngest of five children. She lives with her mother and three of her brothers and sisters. One of her brothers lives in Jamaica and her mother, who is from St Elizabeth, keeps in close contact with family there. She has talked to Marcia a great deal about the island.

Marcia's parents came to Britain together and both found work in factories. When they first arrived they stayed with her father's brother and then moved from house to house for a while before settling in Handsworth. Marcia has lived all her life in Handsworth and Lozells. Her parents split up fairly recently and things have been a bit difficult between Marcia and her mother:

'I'd really like the relationship between us to be good but we don't get on. I think that's a shame. My mum's got her boyfriend now and I don't like him at all. He's been with mum about six months now and I've never had a conversation with him. Just say "hello" and "goodbye" to him and keep out of his way. My brothers and sisters don't get on with him either. My mum doesn't think of us like she used to; it's made me understand how adults can be.'

Marcia sees quite a lot of her father as he lives nearby. She describes him as being very quiet: 'You've got to start the talking to get a conversation." Marcia's dad used to work for British Rail, cleaning trains and looking after stock. He is now unemployed.

Marcia spends a lot of her time at a local youth club; she enjoys mixing with people. She plays netball and volleyball and she has made day trips to London with the club. She would like to be an accountant or a solicitor as she is conscious that there are few Black women in these fields; she is determined to prove that you don't have to be a white man to succeed.

The girls talked about some of the reasons there is a Black community in Britain and recounted some family histories of migration. They compared the experiences of Black people with those of white people in this country. They then described some of the experiences which both Afro-Caribbean and Asian people have and reflected on what it means to be 'mixed race' in a racist society. What does the future hold? They tried to predict what they would be doing in ten years' time.

Why are we here?

Marcia

'I used to wonder why Black people are living here. We've never covered that in history, and that's the point. I had to go and ask my mum. My mum told me that Black people were all shipped over on boats. Working in the factories they wanted Blacks. "Come and work in the factories for us and we'll pay you money", but it's still, sort of, slave labour. To look at it another way, the white people don't think about the Blacks and what they've done, because if it wasn't for the Blacks England wouldn't be like it is now. When Britain had all its colonies it was us who built up the factories, got working, got the materials going and everything . . . And they want to push us out to our own countries! They bring us into it and now they're trying to push us back out.'

Jasbir

'In my old school we had an Indian teacher and she told us that they said to Asian people and Black people that in England the pavements are made of gold and things like that. They were told that they could come here. And then when they did come here they made them work. They treated them as slaves. And yet, when they wanted to grow, say, cotton, because it wasn't hot enough here they used to go to other people's countries and make war on their countries. They wanted everything!'

Elaine
'My grandad told me that he was in the army and the white people used to tell him what to do. Then they sent him here. That's why he's living here now, otherwise he wouldn't have come here.'

Nazrah
'My dad came here before my mum. He came here as a student, studied and then he got married in Pakistan and brought my mum here. That was in 1969. He used to work as a telephone engineer, and then he moved over and bought a shop in Small Heath. He's been working there ever since and saving – putting a little bit away – to move back to Pakistan.'

Marcia
'My mum says the reason why she came to this country is that she was sent. My grandmother and grandfather told her that she had to come over and earn a bit of money. When they needed all those people in England, people thought the money is over there, the money is in England, let's go! They said they needed loads of jobs done in England, so come over and you'll get loads of jobs! But now they've built everything, it's turned out the other way. Now if a Jamaican person goes back over from where they've come from, Jamaicans expect them to have a lot of money. But it doesn't really work out like that. Some of the Jamaicans are better off than the ones that live in England.'

Mumtaz
'My parents are both from Pakistan and my dad came over here about twenty years ago or so, and he worked as a guard on the

railway right from the start. In Pakistan he was in the air force. I think he must have started off in agriculture but I'm not sure. He served as a pilot, then he came over to Britain to have a broader future. My mum came here after my dad had established a house and a future here. She worked as a teacher when she first came here, teaching Urdu, but she gave that up because of the family. My dad's recently lost his job and that has changed a lot in our family. It's affected everybody, I think our friends as well.'

Experience more!

Gillian

'They've got to know about us. We've ventured into England. They've got to venture into Jamaica, America, all over. They've got to experience more. The way I see white people is that they are just living life. Fair enough, they are white, they're living in England, it's a white man's country, they just see themselves as living life. But with Black people we can't just live life. We've got to plan out our life: more or less plan it, stage by stage. They don't really plan out their life – they don't have to. But we have to, we have to try harder.'

Erica

'Except for those people who are really against racism, white people don't understand what it's really about. They expect everything to be easy going for them if they are white. They may have to work hard but we've always got to work hard for what we want to achieve.'

Cover-up

Elaine

'I don't think we do enough about the slave trade in history. They just brush over it. We just do it in passing. We were learning about cotton and there were people in the class laughing at the slaves. And I think we should do more to understand things about Belfast, and the IRA, because that's history as well. And we should study more about South Africa.'

Marcia
'I think what Elaine is saying is right. They block it out because they feel a bit guilty. That's the way I see it. The white teacher feels a bit guilty sometimes, and then you've always got people smirking in class. I asked Mr W last year, "How come we don't do anything on the slave trade? After all that's history isn't it? Why don't we learn about it, or about South Africa? Why just basically England?" OK, we live in England, but it should be about all over the world. And he said that he didn't really know, and that they don't really have any evidence. But they have got evidence. They're just trying to cover it.'

Elaine
'Yes. They're just trying to cover the evidence. First they say that they can't get the books: that they don't publish it because people argue about putting the wrong things in and blocking out other material and being biased. Then the teacher says no because any material about South Africa would definitely be biased. And then the teacher said that they couldn't really do it because it wouldn't be true. But I still think we should study those countries.'

Famous or invisible?

Elaine
'I would like to study Martin Luther King. We've mentioned him once, that is all, just once. He really changed America, didn't he? Yet we spend hours looking at other people like Sir Richard Arkwright.'

Marcia

'All he did was invent a machine, a spinning or weaving machine, and look what Martin Luther King did for Black people. They overlook him because he's Black, and he was American. I personally think that if they tried to express any of Martin Luther King's views in school they would get it wrong and there would be arguments. They'd hide things, they definitely would.

'It's not just school, of course. One day in the holidays there was a programme on television called "Open Air". Someone phoned in, I don't know if they were Black or white, but they were saying, "What about Mary Seacole? She played as important a part as Florence Nightingale. How come there hasn't been anything about her on a history programme?" There was a guy answering who makes history programmes, and he was saying something about history books, that the material is not in them, but that they would be touching on the subject in the near future.'

Everyone's history

Marcia

'But I think we should all be doing Black history and Indian history and more world history in school, because when we touch on the issues everyone starts laughing. They show pictures of India and cotton and everyone starts laughing. We touch on something about slavery and everyone is laughing. I didn't see anything that was funny. If that's their reaction it's more important still that we should be studying these things. It is history and if we want to be taught history then these things should be included.'

Cynthia

'One of the problems is that some white kids do feel guilty about it. Some of them feel guilty and some of them ask, "Why should it happen?" Some people feel guilty, some people don't. It would help everyone if they employed more Black teachers.'

Two different worlds

Gillian
'I think that what Salman Rushdie says about Britain being two entirely different worlds is true. I don't see white people saying different things to Black people and Asian. Of course there are certain differences between us, but as far as I'm concerned if someone asked me "How do you see an Asian person?" I'd say like my brother or sister, because to me they are Black. I'm around a lot of Asian people and I enjoy their company, not because of their colour, but because of what they are. That's how I see things.'

Elaine
'White people may see things differently to the way Black people see them. I think it is two different worlds for some people. There are some white people willing to fight racism, but I don't think there are a lot of people. I think there are some people who are more openly racist to Asian people than to other Black people.'

Afia
'White people don't know what our lives are like. Say someone makes racist remarks. You can't really go up to an English person and say, oh, that another white person said that to me, you just can't say that. They don't know what it's like. And even if you do say it to them it won't mean anything to them because they're still white.'

Marcia
'I think that in one sense it isn't two entirely different worlds because in many cases nowadays whites will get on with Blacks

or Asians. Now you see a lot of mixed families. In Liverpool, where you see a lot of mixed families, it's not two entirely different worlds. In some parts of Liverpool there's absolutely mixed races so obviously the whites get on with the Blacks, but in some places like Sutton you've got whites who are the majority in the area and one or two Blacks on the outskirts of what's going on, so in that sense it remains two different experiences and two different worlds.'

Erica

'Again it boils down to school, what they teach you, what they choose to teach you. Shouldn't they just tell us what our rights are in school and outside school? When you go out and you're refused something you just accept it. When you think someone is being racist, but you're not sure where you stand, you just take it. What are you supposed to do? If you are made aware of what you can do and of what the law says then it would be all right. You could voice your opinions. They expect you to shut up and not do anything, and if you do do something they accuse you of causing trouble.'

Mumtaz

'I think that it's true that Britain is two different worlds. Where you have Black people you have all the Black people in one community, and where you have whites you tend to have all whites in one community as well. There are certain areas, in Birmingham and all over the country, that are known as "white areas" and others which are known as "Black areas". If a Black person moves into a white area there can be lots of prejudice shown until they have to move from there because of all the racism they're given. It's not apartheid, but some people have suggested something like that. In England! I think that's ridiculous because the situation in South Africa is really outrageous. If they went towards that here I would definitely move. You see on TV what's happening in South Africa and you really feel for the Black people.'

Afia

'I think that the "two different worlds" is right. What Mumtaz is saying about the communities is true: Handsworth is meant for the Blacks and Solihull is meant for the whites. But it's sad. We're coming into the 1990s and you shouldn't have things like apartheid, racism, famine in Africa and everything. It should be all gone. We should be thinking about what to do with the country, and with the world we live in. More and more problems are being created and it's becoming harder on everybody.'

Mixed feelings

Gillian

'Most white people see people of mixed backgrounds as Black whatever their complexion, even if they are fair skinned. If you've got a brown complexion they'd say that you can go back with the Blacks or the Asians.'

Elaine

'I've noticed that some people give me and my mum dirty looks when we're out together – she's white. And a lot of Black men have said to my dad that he should stick to his own kind, and they've been really nasty about white people.'

Marcia

'For me, as a Black person, when I see a mixed race person I treat them as a Black person. I can't really push them aside and say "Oh, you're white or you're half caste". Elaine or anyone else, I treat them as Black people. I recognize they have a white parent and I accept them for who they are.'

Cynthia

'There are some mixed race people who don't like to be classed
as Black. They say, "I'm not Black, I'm brown". The same is
true of some Asians. They are Black but they don't want to
admit that they're Black. It's because of some kind of fear of
saying, "I'm Black". We live in a racist society.'

Elaine

'I hang around with a lot of white people and they seem to me
to have a problem about this. Marcia's quite clear about it: she
sees me as Black. The first person who said "Afro-Caribbean"
to me, I didn't know what she was talking about! I just said to
her, "I'm Black!" A lot of my white friends say, "No you're not
Black, I see you as white." I really feel like screaming, saying:
"I'm not white, I'm Black!"'

'Sometimes they are calling everybody names around me,
using words like "nigger" and I look at them and they say,
"Oh, God, I didn't mean anything." Sometimes it really causes
some bad arguments around me and sometimes I just say,
"Forget it!" When people say "Paki" I really start arguing, I
really start getting involved. My mum told me I must learn not
to react like that, but I can't stand it when someone says, "I
didn't mean to be racist, but . . ."'

Tara

'I've got a friend who's Black but some people mistake her for
white, because she's mixed. They talk to her but when they
know what colour she really is they don't want to know her. So
it's not easy.'

Jasbir

'If a white guy fancies someone who's a different colour, they
will say "Paki-lover" and all this. If you see them waking down
the street with someone a different colour they will all start
calling them names.'

Nazrah

'I want to explain something about my dad. My dad's a
shopkeeper, we've got a shop and we live on top of it. We
sometimes get difficult customers in the shop. This Black man
came into the shop and my dad had recently been in hospital
because they had had a fight. That man came in and he was
bugging my dad. You know, "How much is this?" and "How
much is that?" My dad is really prejudiced against Blacks and
he doesn't believe in equality at all. You should hear him. You
wouldn't believe it! My best friend is Afro-Caribbean and we
once had a party and I invited her, along with all our Asian
friends. All the Asian friends there were all going on in our
own language and making her feel really uncomfortable: "Look
at your friend" and "Is that your friend?" But in some ways we
have a lot in common with Afro-Caribbean girls. They get
bugged like we do with racial prejudice, and we can put our
thoughts together.'

Rasheeda

'If there were whites here it would probably be difficult to say
what we want to. I think it's important for girls to have
opportunities to talk to each other like this because in that way
they get to know more. If they are faced by anything they can
actually solve the problem, because they can know what other
people have done and what they feel. It's easier to share things
with Afro-Caribbean girls because although I don't know
anything about their religion I'd probably have a lot in
common with them because they're Black as well. They may be
Christians and therefore linked to whites, but if a girl is Black
she will be faced by as much racism, so in that sense we're the
same. It might be difficult to talk about the culture and the
religion. All Blacks are the same, they share a lot, Afro-
Caribbean, Asians, Hindus, Muslims, or whatever, because
they are all Black. The great division is between us and the
whites, not between the Blacks themselves.'

Gillian

'I train at a swimming club and there are a lot of Asian people there. I just happened to be walking with four of them, and this Black guy turned round and said, "Oh no, what are you turning into, a Paki-lover?" I told him, "Look it's none of your business, whatever I do is mine." He went to grab hold of me, but because they treat me in the club as one of their sisters they whacked him one. Now when he sees me he always calls me "Paki-lover". For him to say that is wrong. But when I challenged him he just said, "Why don't you stick to your own kind?" I asked him "Why does it have to be a 'kind'?"'

Type cast

Afia

'Because you're an Asian you've got to work hard because you're cast as an Asian. I was talking to my dad about my plans for the future and he says, "You've got to think about where you're living and you've got to think about who you are." That's important. But then he says, "The kind of job you want is not right. The only suitable job for an Asian woman is that of a pharmacist or an accountant. And you've got to think about what your husband is going to think when you get married, and about what your in-laws are going to think." I don't think that's right. You are Asian but I think you should be able to do what you want to do.'

Rasheeda

'I always tell my parents I want to continue studying. My dad may let me but he's worried about what people may think. I don't think that's right. I'm not sure I'll be able to do what I want to do, and that's not fair.'

In ten years' time . . .

Mumtaz

'In ten years' time I think I'd like to have a comfortable job – not married – and, I think, working my way up because I want to start as a legal executive and then work my way up to a solicitor. I don't know where I'm going to go from there. I think at twenty-five I'll probably be doing lots of exams even though I hate exams, and probably be working and trying to get a comfortable living.

'I want my future here in Britain, I don't really know what it's like in Pakistan. I was only about six when I visited and I can't remember very much except that it was so green. I consider Britain to be my country as well, because I was born here. We haven't got any other relatives here so we're really on our own. We didn't have any relatives to fall back on when my dad lost his job, so we've had to start from scratch. That's why I think my future here in Britain is important. That's why I want to get my education, try to set up in something that I'm interested in as a career here and then go on from there.'

Afia

'In ten years' time I'll hopefully have something to do with the fashion business. I'll have a shop and be working my way up. I probably will be married and have a child and things like that. But even though I may be married I would still like to make design my career and go as high as possible.'

Nazrah

'Hopefully I'll be working and maybe studying. Possibly married I should think.'

Rasheeda

'Well, no matter what my parents say I'm definitely going to read on and get what I want, which is a career. But in ten years' time I'll probably be married and living in Pakistan. I might think there's not much point in my career, because what am I going to do there? Probably just live as a housewife. Well, I'm going to try not to let that happen and I still want to continue my career, do my job and everything. I'm not very worried about marriage but I don't really want to get married.'

Elaine
'I want to go on to college but I'm not sure after that.'

Tara
'Perhaps study law, I know it's hard but I'd still like to try. Otherwise I'd like to work in an airport, I know I'd have to work nights but I don't mind working and I like going out. Hopefully I'd become an air stewardess. I don't like staying in one place, I'd like to go to different countries and move around.'

Satnam
'I want to work with children when I leave school, because when you go to nursery school you mostly see white teachers and assistants there.'

Jasbir
'Either something to do with computers or something to do with photography, I'm not sure yet.'

Gillian
'I've got three ambitions that I'd like to try. First I'd like to become a probation officer, that's what I'd really like to do. Then, this might sound sexist, but I'd like to open a club for women so that they have somewhere that would help them overcome the difficulties that they have. And I would really like to go on TV.'

Pauline

'I'd like to be a nurse or a doctor. My grandmother was a midwife in Jamaica and right from when I was little I've always wanted to be a nurse or a doctor.'

Angela

'I want to be an engineer or a mechanic. I think I'll have a few problems because probably if a girl is working in a place doing that kind of job then the men might not like it.'

Arina

'I'd like to become a civil servant, but the thing I really want to do before I settle down to a career is to travel. I like being on my own, and when I'm in Birmingham whenever I want to get out of the house I just catch a bus up and down anywhere around the city. People say I love travelling too much. My mum is taking me to America this summer. She says if I like it and if I get on with our relations there she will arrange for me to go to school there when the rest of the family goes to Bangladesh.'

Erica

'I don't know what I'll be doing in ten years' time, but I'd like to go to college and train to be an accountant.'

Anita

'I want to go to university and study law. I'd like to be a barrister. When you look at cases in courts and you look at Black women, you see they don't always get justice. Sometimes they can't afford good lawyers and even when they can they will probably be white.'

Cynthia

'I'd like to be an actress or a TV presenter. You might see me in ten years' time taking Selina Scott's place!'

Marcia

'Like Cynthia I'd also like to be on TV, probably acting or presenting a show. One of my ambitions is to be an accountant, but I know it's hard work. I would also quite like to be a solicitor because I've realized that there are not many Black solicitors and not many women. If I was able to become a solicitor I'd be able to prove to people that we can do it. Black women can be solicitors, you don't have to be white, you don't have to be a man.'

6:
Family feelings

■■■■■■■■■■■■■■■■■■■■■■■■■■■■■■■■■■■■■■■

Most of us have strong feelings about our families. Whether we accept or reject our parents' views, their lives tend to influence ours in a significant way.

Children's books, magazines, television and advertising portray a 'normal' or 'typical' family, which probably consists of a mother, a father, and an average of two children. This bears little relationship to reality. Despite the fact that Black families are almost completely ignored (how many times have you seen an advertisement for cornflakes which shows a Black family sitting down to breakfast together, or one for washing powder showing a Black mother and her children?) another set of stereotypes exist about Black women in relationship to family roles. These stereotypes are very different for Afro-Caribbean and Asian women, but can act as strong pressures on Black girls growing up in Britain today.

Wherever the pattern of Black women's lives have differed from that of white women, the white pattern has been presented as the norm. Here the girls reflect on their experiences within their families and respond to these and to the false images of themselves which they encounter in the wider community.

Gillian

Gillian was born in Birmingham but has travelled quite a bit, living for a while in the United States and in Jamaica. Her mother was born in America and came to live in Britain at the age of nine.

Gillian's mother's family are Roman Catholics and are of mixed descent. Some of them refused to have anything to do with Gillian's mother when she chose to marry someone darker skinned. Gillian's father's family are from Jamaica and they are Seventh Day Adventists.

Gillian is the youngest in the family and lives with her parents and one of her sisters. Her mother is a nurse and her father works as a coach driver. Gillian has strong views on many subjects and is very outspoken. This has landed her in some trouble at school; she says of school, 'I don't like it very much, but I try to get the most out of it.' She is a member of a swimming club and spends a lot of her spare time training. Gillian is very clear about what she wants for the future:

'My ambition, my one great ambition, is to make it known that Black people can get somewhere. I don't think that Black children in care are treated very well, and the few Black social workers that we get are in positions where they can't help Black children. I'd like to help change things. Also not many women in social work get into high positions, which I hope to gain. I want to be out there to show that women, and that Black women, can really do something.'

Tara

Tara is the eldest in her family and she lives with her father and two of her sisters. Her parents are divorced and the younger children live with Tara's mother. Tara does not see her mother, whom she blames for the break-up of the family. She is a quiet girl who has quite a few friends but who remains reserved in company.

The family are Hindus and Tara's father runs a post office. Tara shares quite a lot of responsibility with her grandmother, looking after her sisters and supporting them in their interests. She has very fond memories of visiting her family in New Delhi when she was a small girl and in some ways she thinks of India as home. She gave examples of particular difficulties that Asian girls in Britain may face:

'When we go up town me and my sister are very conscious that we're surrounded by white people and they're surprised to see us going shopping. They don't expect to see two Asian girls of our age buying clothes on their own. Where we live it's different. There are a lot of Asian people and most of them agree that Asian boys in the area are a nuisance. Every Asian girl has to watch them, they can behave like sex maniacs, following you home and everything. Sometimes we have problems with them. Even on the bus this boy came and hit me for no reason at all. I hit him back and he was amazed. He just walked off in shame and everyone was laughing at him.'

As a result of her parents' break-up Tara has strong views about marriage. She thinks it most unlikely that she will get married because so many marriages fail: 'It's not really worth getting married in the first place if you're going to end up getting divorced.' Tara's parents had an arranged marriage but since his own marriage ended Tara's father is reluctant to arrange marriages for his daughters, recognizing that Asian marriages face particular stresses in a British context. Tara is free to make up her own mind about this in the future.

Tara is not certain what she would like to do with her life but would like either to take up some kind of legal career or work in an airport.

Rasheeda

Rasheeda lives in Moseley. The family are Muslims and Rasheeda, who is the eldest of five, carries considerable responsibility at home for housework and childcare. She is a quiet girl who enjoys netball and other sports at school, and who spends any spare time at home reading:

'I like reading non-fiction because I like finding out about things. I love nature, I'm really mad about it. I've got a small kitten. And I enjoy watching television, documentary films mostly.'

Rasheeda's family have arranged a marriage for her with her cousin, who lives in Pakistan. He is studying engineering and they will not marry until he is finished. Since it is quite a long course Rasheeda hopes that she will be able to continue her studies. She is very clear about what she wants to do which is to study medicine or some related subject. After that she says she will be happy to marry her cousin and to live with him in Pakistan. She loves Pakistan which is where she was born:

'It's a beautiful place. Our family live in a village there. It's so open, there are so many fields, and you can live out in the open and go up onto the roof of the house.'

Rasheeda is given very little personal freedom by her parents:

'I'd love to go anywhere. I wouldn't care as long as I'm out of the house. Because I haven't been out for so long now I'm used to it. The only time I ever go out is to the library, which is every Saturday. And that's it.

'I'm looking forward to the future. In the end I'll tell my parents what I want to do. I think my dad will understand because he's quite a soft character. It's my mum who's strict. I'll make sure that I do what I want and not what they want, because I'm going to spend a life afterwards and I'm not expecting to spend it unhappy just because of them, because of their decisions. So I'm going to make my decisions myself.'

In the discussions on families the girls looked at their positions in the family and that of their brothers, and talked about their parents' expectations of them. They reflected on society's image of Asian women and challenged it through examples in their own lives. Several girls of different religions and cultural backgrounds explained what the practice of arranged marriage meant to them. Discussion on families led to a conversation about religion, and the girls finished by talking about their mothers and their relationships with them.

No equality

Jasbir

'Boys can get away with a lot more than girls in my family. My brother, although he's only nine, I can guarantee that by the time he's sixteen he'll have more freedom than me or my sisters. He'll be able to go out with his friends and that kind of thing. There are already differences. My brother can get his hair cut and we can't. My dad used to wear a turban but then when he came to England he had his hair cut. We're always asking my mum why, if my dad can get his hair cut, we can't. If he were wearing a turban then that would be a different thing. We wouldn't really mind. Our brother can have his hair cut, and we just want to expect things like that. But our parents want things to be more traditional for their daughters than they do for the boys in the family.

'I use any opportunity to take my freedom. Last year we were attacked one day walking home. Some boys poured some kind of tar on us. Of course I was upset with all this awful stuff in my hair but afterwards I used that as a way of getting my hair cut. Some girls are happy with the amount of freedom that their parents give them, and if they were given more they wouldn't use it. I think that if I have any chance of greater freedom then I'll jump at it.

'It really depends on the parents. In our house they are really strict. It's not really a question of culture because some Indian parents don't mind so much. At home I'm not really supposed to wear skirts. I try to get away with it if I can but it doesn't often work. Some girls I know have their hair cut, spiked, you name it, but most can't. You hear of all these girls who are running away, but it's got to be something serious between a girl and her family to make her do that. There is a refuge where Indian girls can go if they run away and I think it's run by Asian women.'

Fixed image

Nazrah
'I think one of the problems is that white people have a fixed image of Asian women. They would listen to what one girl has to say about her family and assume that all Asian women are the same. It may have something to do with the clothes we wear, so that when they see an Asian woman in traditional dress that affects their view.'

Afia
'I don't think that should affect our choice of clothes though. I think that Asians should wear traditional dress whenever we want to because if you had whites going to India and Pakistan they wouldn't want to wear what we were wearing, they'd probably wear their own skirts or whatever.'

Mumtaz
'I think the image that white people have of Asian women especially is that they are all housewives with about ten kids and that they are stuck in the house making the dinner all day. All they ever do is have babies, make the dinner and that's it. They think that other Black women are coming up in the world

now, getting better jobs and having more choices. Many Asian women want to be with their families so they find it hard to have jobs. There are no really easy choices. The problem is that they see us as all being the same. People think they're just housewives and leave it at that.'

Nazrah

'A lot of white people think that Asian men are very sexist and that they don't treat women very fairly. I expect as many white men are equally sexist, but perhaps it shows in different ways. Many Asian men have been brought up in a culture where the wife does all the housework and doesn't go out for a job, but in the modern parts of Pakistan and India men are brought up differently, and so the men have different attitudes. Asian culture is developing in different ways and here in Britain many men know that their wives want to go out to work and do so. They accept that.'

Afia

'Women must stand up for themselves. They cope with a lot, they have babies and they put up with a lot of troubles in life with men. Women don't get a lot of what they deserve. All women must stand up for themselves, whether they are Asian or English or whatever. Whoever you are, it doesn't really matter, you must be prepared to support other women.'

Dutiful daughters take the blame

Mumtaz

'Rasheeda's the eldest and it's hard for her at home because of that. My sister, who's the eldest, has a lot of responsibility. She's expected to lead the way for the rest of us. She didn't pass all her exams, and then my next sister didn't either. My eldest sister got all the blame because she was meant to take responsibility for teaching the rest. She has to look after the whole family and she doesn't get as much time as she would like for her own studies. You do have more responsibility placed on you if you are the eldest, and it's harder, much harder, if you are a girl.'

Gillian

'At home I'm expected to do a lot of things around the house. My brother gets away with doing next to nothing. When I've finished I'm allowed to go out but I always have a certain time when I must be back.'

Cynthia

'I think my mum likes the boys more. They have a lot more freedom. When I go out I must say at what time I'll be home, but they'll say they'll be back at ten and come home at twelve or one. She expects them to wash up and if they make a mess they have to clean it up, so it can be fair, but most of the time they get away with it. Sometimes my dad tells me I have to do something, and I tell him he has to pay me if he wants the job done, and he does!'

Marcia

'My brother is nineteen, and sometimes he doesn't come in until the morning when I'm in bed sleeping. I used to say, "You're lucky!" But girls are more likely to get attacked than boys, so that at one stage my mum wouldn't give me a key because she thought I wouldn't come in at the right time. My parents aren't strict, but in a way I prefer to get in earlier than my brother, because that's the decent thing to do. That's the way I see it. I should come in earlier than my brothers because I'm the youngest.'

Guarding *izzat*

Nazrah

'At home we're different, but when we go out we're expected to behave in a certain way. It's the same between Britain and Pakistan. Here we can do things which our parents wouldn't expect us to do if we were in Pakistan. In Pakistan we'll be expected to act in a more ladylike and disciplined way. When we are at home here we can relax and be ourselves. But when we go out people can look at us and tell other people about our behaviour. News passes fast. At home we can be wild ones, hitting whichever of our brothers and sisters go past, and telling each other to shut up! When we go to someone's house we don't do that. It's got a lot to do with reputation.

'Sometimes, if I've had an argument with my parents, I feel like shouting out: "All you care about is the reputation!" because arguments are always about something which has happened in front of somebody. With Asian families reputation is the first thing because if you've got a bad reputation nobody wants to know you. You've got to keep that reputation going. It's very important for girls because when the time comes for them to get married if they've been seen to behave well then that will be an extra boost if they want to get married to a particular person.

'*Izzat* means "reputation", "honour", the same thing. In Asian families it's the thing. The woman takes more responsibility for *izzat* than the man. If you get followed by boys, for example, most Asian parents are likely to blame it on the girls not the boys. They might swear at the boys but you get looks of disapproval from your parents. My dad will shout at the boys but my mum will look at us, give us dirty looks saying, "You've called them upon us."

'You see the same thing in Indian films. If someone gets raped they get chucked out of the house. It's not, "Oh, the poor thing, she needs some care and attention now." It's "Get out! We don't want you anymore!" I don't know if that would be the case in our family, but I've watched the films and taken notice. First they are really loving to their daughters and after they get raped they just kick them out. God, they're really horrible doing that. The woman that it's happened to, she goes down and down and has to face all these bad things. And they don't have places where you can go to, like they have here, women's associations, they don't have anything. They just roam the streets and think of killing themselves until someone rescues them and tries to hide what's happened to them. Suddenly it all comes out because, whatever happens, it always sticks. Sometime or other it comes out.

'If someone went out with a boy that would be another thing which would damage *izzat*. Someone's bound to see you if you're in town and then the gossip would be everywhere. It would get to the parents and the parents would be mad.'

People will talk!

Marcia
'Parents are more worried about the daughters than the sons. I've really noticed because my brother's nineteen, four years older than me, but at one stage he could have anyone coming to the house. He could have three girls knocking on the door. If I'd have had three guys knocking on the door it would be: "What are they doing there? Do you want to show me up? People will talk! They'll be saying how come your daughter's got so many guys!" My brother could have so many coming and going and me lucky to get away with one! So girls' reputations count for a lot more.'

Cynthia
'If my brother's girlfriend phones up when my mum is at home she might ask "Who's that?" but that's it. One time I was

having a conversation with a friend about a boy and everyone
was listening. My brother said "Well I know you fancy him",
and everybody was joining in saying, "I know you fancy him.
Shame!" It became everyone's business!'

Angela

'When I want to bring a boyfriend to the house I just say,
"Mum, I want to bring a friend here." She'll say, "What kind
of friend?" and when I say it's a boy she'll just say, "Oh". Then
afterwards she just settles down. She's quite strict because she
grew up in Jamaica and her mum was quite strict.'

Gillian

'On this subject things get very tense in my family. I can't have
any boys calling at the door even to lend them an English book.
I can't have anyone phoning up. I can't really say I'm bringing
somebody home just as a friend. I can't do that at all. I have
my own friends and they're just friends but my parents
wouldn't see it as that. I've said before that I train with a lot of
guys and at first that's probably why my dad didn't want me to
train. I don't really hang around with a lot of girls and my
mum has noticed that and she's a bit wary of it. I had a phone
call the other day and she was really fuming, she was really
questioning me about it. In the end she found out it was my
instructor. She didn't listen to me at first. My dad went off the
handle. "Who's this? What are you doing? How old is he?" He
really went mad. Some people say that Asian girls have a lot of
restrictions put on their freedom but in fact most families are
worried about their daughters at one time or another.'

Dressed up to go nowhere

Cynthia

'Boys do have more freedom. My brothers can go out anywhere
but when I get dressed up my mum says, "Where are you

going? How come you're all dressed up?" Once I was just going to town but my brother was saying, "She's meeting her boyfriend." I wasn't even going out with anyone! "Mum," I said, "I'm just going to town to get some hair-do, I'm not meeting anyone, I promise you." "I don't care, you're not going!" Another time I did go to town. My sister made up this lie. My mum thought it was true. My sister said that I had met this guy up town and that we went to McDonalds. My sister said "I saw her sitting in McDonalds staring into this boy's eyes!" I was laughing but my mum thought it was serious and she said, "Right, that's the last time you go out!"

'That was about a year ago. She lets me go up to town now. Sometimes she knows I'm meeting my friends but she doesn't really like me to go with my friends. She prefers me to go by myself. I don't know why.'

Satnam

'Cynthia's mum sounds a bit like mine. If I was seeing somebody I think my mum would go mad and keep me in the house. She'd probably check up on me at school too.'

Nazrah

'I think I'll have to become more broad-minded. I'm very critical of girls who go out. They look strict the way they wear traditional dress and they come to school with scarves on their heads and no make-up, and with their hair tied back. As soon as they get to school they take their hair out, take their socks off and put high heeled sandals on. They get dressed up to go out of school at lunch time. I've got a friend like this and I ask her why she does it and she just won't answer me. I think they do it just to show off, just to say to other girls, "Look, I've got a boyfriend, you haven't, that makes me better than you. That makes me more likeable, more popular." But they are taking quite big risks, because some of them come from good families and if their parents found out they'd kill them. They'd beat

them and they'd kick them out of the house. It's a question of
reputation or *izzat* and they're bound to find out.'

Afia

'But the boys that these girls are meeting are Asian boys. Their
reputation is never at risk. If a boy has been seen with lots of
different girls then it could be a problem, but if he's only seen
with one girl that's all right. But if a girl is seen with a boy and
her parents get to hear about it they would go mad.'

Nazrah

'I don't think my brother would ever do that, but if he did
when he was older I think he'd be let off easily. I don't know
what my mum would do but my dad would talk to him.

'It's the same prejudice that women face in all cultures.
English people get the impression that women are really
downgraded in Asian families but it's just the opposite in many
ways because at home they can do anything. It's the respect
and reputation that's the sexist part of it. At home they rule the
house and get all the money that the husband brings from
work.'

Tara

'My father doesn't really worry about me. He says there's not
much difference between girls and boys. He says that we
should be treated equally.'

Freedom and trust

Mumtaz

'I think that I get a lot of freedom from my parents because I
can go out whenever I want to. But I tend to choose not to. If I
want to go to town I can, even by myself, but I'll go with my
sister usually. I think that my dad trusts us more than my

mum. I think that mums always have this kind of funny feeling about their children. They think that their sons are everything, especially in Asian families, and they trust their sons so much and really the sons go behind their backs and deceive them. Whereas the daughters, they have to prove to their parents that they can be trusted and so work harder at developing that trust with them. So I think my parents give me a lot of freedom, but I choose not to be outrageous and go everywhere every minute of the day and stay out late at night. But I think if I was like that my parents would put a stop to it.'

Anita

'I have a sister who left home at seventeen because she didn't really get on with my parents. They found her and she came back after two months because my grandmother in India was ill and was asking for my mother. My mother went to India and my sister came home and looked after us, but after a couple of months she left home again because nothing had really changed. She gave my parents a chance to change.

'Things are better for me because now that I'm the only one left at home my dad takes time to talk to me and we get on much better than he did with the older ones. I know that if I had any sort of disagreement with my parents my sister would support me. She'd give practical advice on where I could stay and what sort of benefit I could get, and she'd support me morally. She'd back me up. She'd give her opinions and she'd tell me whether she thought I was right or wrong but even if she thought I was wrong she'd still support me in making my own decisions and give me logical advice.'

Religion

Anita

'My parents are very strict Hindus. Since my sister left home my parents have become really religious. We have a shrine and lots of pictures of gods. My mum lights the *diva* (lamp) every day. She's always done that, she used to do it when I was little. She holds it around the gods. She's always fasted once a week, my dad only started when my sister left. It doesn't mean so much to me because religion just came into my life all of a sudden. Before that they gave me no religious training and then about the age of twelve or thirteen things changed. Now my mum is always bringing God's name into everything. I find it hard to make sense of some of their beliefs.'

Gillian

'We've got two religions in my family. My dad's a Seventh Day Adventist but I don't follow that, I never have; my mum's a Catholic and I followed that when I was younger. All of us children apart from two of my sisters are Catholics. To us religion means everlasting life. It's something that you don't have to practise, it's always there. God is everywhere. If there's something in the Catholic religion that I don't believe in, when I'm at church I back down on these things. For example, no child should be aborted, you mustn't go on the pill, and you can't get married more than once. I don't believe in it really. You're not supposed to hurt another person. That's true, I believe that, but why bring another person into the world if you are going to hurt them? Going on the pill is preventing all the trouble but in our religion it's a disgrace. The older people in church make it sound like it's really wrong.

'Religion to me is supposed to mean peace and harmony and helping everyone else. Basically I still follow it and it's something that makes me relax. I can think about what happens, why I'm here, and things like that. A lot of people say to me, "Why can't you do certain things in the Catholic religion?" and they tell me that this is wrong. Well, there are rules that I can follow and that I don't because in my own mind they're wrong. Some people say, "Well if you don't follow it how can you say you're a Catholic?" Those questions I've asked myself over and over and I still can't answer them. My mum says I'll just have to carry on and find out when I'm older.

'We've got a really ancient poem which is about footprints and it expresses what I feel God is and what we are. A man has a dream and he sees the scenes of his life before him and he sees two sets of footprints in the sand. At certain times in his life he sees only one set and he questions it and the Lord replies, "When you saw one set of footprints it was when I carried you." That's how I feel when people ask me.'

Cynthia

'My family are Christians. They belong to the New Testament Church of God. Like Gillian's family they are quite strict on religion. They expect me to be very different from Marcia, for example. They expect me to stay in the house, not go out, and just do what I'm supposed to do. I just don't do it. I think that it's my life and that I should choose. It must be my decision. I think that as far as religion goes that if your parents choose something it doesn't automatically mean that you have to do it too. If your parents are Christian it doesn't mean you're Christian. You don't have to be one, and if your parents are Catholic it doesn't mean you have to be a Catholic.'

Marcia

'No one in my family is really religious. When I was younger all of my family used to go to church, my mum, my dad, my sister and all of us. We don't go anymore. I feel that religion is stronger than racism, somehow. When you get religious wars, religious fighting, it's as powerful as racism, because people have got their religion to back them to say what they are fighting against is wrong. It's wrong when religions set themselves up against each other, it's wrong that they should cause problems.'

Gillian

'Religion is a powerful thing and some people become possessed with it: they say they can't do something because of their religion and they become really inflexible. Other people are more relaxed and they think each thing through and they don't go by every vow and every word. They may go to church every Sunday, but they don't take all they're told so much to heart. They question. It goes both ways.

'Many Catholics believe that if you marry someone, not necessarily outside the Catholic religion, but someone who is not religious, that you're not really married. Some believe that if you're not married in a Catholic church you're not properly married. I think you should be able to marry who you want and where you want, but really the Catholic religion doesn't encourage you to think like that.'

Elaine

'My mum and my grandad are Jehovah's witnesses. My nan used to go to church a lot and we used to go with her. We're not really religious, that is we believe, but we don't go to church and it's not strict. We always had loads of bibles, and we used to go to Sunday School. I suppose I share the same views as my parents on religion.'

Gillian

'In Birmingham you've got some churches which are largely white and then you've got some which are almost entirely Black. I think it's wrong in a way because why should you split people up according to their colour. People can question the colour of God, but no one knows so it's no good saying well, God's Black so we'll have a Black church, and vice versa. Many Black people were not made very welcome in the churches when they first came to this country, but we should all try to come together as Christians because it's supposed to be peaceful. People are hypocrites within their religion as well.

They make out that God's supposed to have made it this way, but they've made the barrier there themselves.'

Satnam
'We're Sikhs, but you wouldn't describe us as a very religious family. We go to the temple sometimes. It's not on a regular basis, just about once a month. Religion is not really discussed at home. Religion to us probably means having somebody that we can look upon. My dad didn't used to wear a turban but he wears one now. He doesn't like the idea of going to the temple. I can't see the point of him wearing a turban if he doesn't want to go.

'His friends persuaded him to wear one and they gave him one and they would have felt bad if he didn't wear it. My mum really didn't want him to wear one because she has to wash it and everything. She's always moaning at him, saying "Why have you got a turban?"'

Jasbir
'My family go to the same temple as Satnam's. My granny and my mum, I think that they probably take it seriously, but my dad doesn't really. My little brother and sister go when my mum goes. Me and my sister will go if it's a wedding, there's one coming up in two weeks, and I went to another a couple of weeks ago. Otherwise I haven't been for months.'

Arina
'My family is not very religious but we believe in Islam. I don't feel very strongly about religion but I think it's important to know something about your religion and your background.'

Tara
'My grandparents are very religious, but my dad isn't at all. Me and my sisters don't really go to the temple, except for weddings.'

107

Arranged marriage

The practice of arranged marriage is often presented as an explanation for the oppression of Asian girls and for conflict between Asian parents and their daughters. Newspaper stories tell sensational stories of girls forced into marriages against their will, and present Asian girls as torn between two separate lives: one living unhappily at home and another at school envying the greater freedom of their white friends. The stereotypical picture is of a girl caught between two cultures, at home in neither. The stereotype gives a very distorted picture of the tradition of arranged marriage and hides the wide range of relationships which can exist between an Asian girl and her parents. The nine Asian girls who feature in this book tell nine different stories which reflect similarities and differences in their situations. The three comments here reflect a variety of experiences and attitudes.

Jasbir
'The thing about arranged marriage is whether or not you see the person and have a chance to make your own mind up about him. In the past you didn't usually see the person and when a girl got married you and your parents and everybody would feel bad. Now you phone him and he phones you and you get to meet and everything. Before no one would allow it. My cousin was going to have an arranged marriage with this guy and she didn't expect to see him. She was really surprised because he wanted her to go out with him for a drink. His family let them go, they wanted them to go out which was really surprising. None of her other cousins knew because they all would have been talking. It was at night that they went out and they had a drink and a chat. My cousin and her parents were really surprised, she even told me and my sister. She made us promise not to tell anyone, not even my mum. Well,

when my mum got married, first she was told that she was getting married to my dad and then they saw each other at the wedding. They didn't even know what each other looked like! They've got a happy marriage. It depends really, because some marriages work out and some don't. It's the same for arranged marriages as for any other.

'If my parents arranged a marriage for me I think they would choose someone in this country. There's usually something with the immigration laws which makes it difficult to marry a boy from India. Either they won't let him come or he'll have to go back at some time during his life, so they'll arrange it in England.'

Anita
'I have mixed feelings about arranged marriage. I know that a higher proportion of arranged marriages work out than love marriages. The issue for me is not whether or not you should have an arranged marriage but whether you should have choice. There is the question of whether you want to get married at all. To me it seems rather crude that at a certain age they should want you to marry a bloke and that it should be a certain type of person. My older sister had an arranged marriage, and she was about twenty-three. I was about six at that time, and I remember them being worried about finding a bloke at the right sort of age because a lot of Indian girls get married younger than that.'

Mumtaz
'I'm not going to get married until I'm over twenty-five. My mum got married when she was twenty-three. Most people think that Pakistani brides are all married at sixteen or seventeen, but with my mum and dad it was different and they both had the chance of an education and a job first. If I get married it will be after I've finished my education and after I've set up in a career. I think I will agree to whoever

my parents choose for me because that's the way it is in our religion and I accept that. If the man is awful, if he's stupid or has a hopeless future then I'll probably object, but I think my parents will ask me first and if I don't like their choice they'll look again.'

Mothers

Afia
'My relationship with my mother, like any other relationship, has its good and bad side. I can talk to her but not as much as I would like to. She approves of my interest in fashion design, but still concerns herself with what people will say. She trusts me, which is good, but she has been in a lot of pain and she doesn't really understand that so have my brother and I. It's as a result of the upsets between my parents. She's adapted to western life because we are here but we will never forget our culture.'

Marcia
'Since my mum's got a boyfriend my life has changed quite a lot. It's made me grow up and be independent. At one stage I'd be quite happy to stay in and watch the telly and do what I want, but since he comes round he determines what happens. He's always there watching golf, boxing or snooker. One minute we'll be watching EastEnders and the next he'll come in and turn it over and say, "Ah, that's better". I just have to walk out of the room I get so mad.

'He knows I don't like him. I have tried to get on with him for my mum's sake. Once I tried smiling at him but . . . well, I just looked at him and I couldn't. My mum doesn't see my point, that I'm trying to help her, and she says, "You've got no manners, you haven't. You should have respect for him." And I say, "Mum, you know I've got respect and everything." The way she goes on I just end up saying, "I know you're on his side and I'm not really bothered." We'll end up having an argument and I'll just go out.

'Some nights it's just so tense when my mum and her boyfriend are there. I'll be doing my homework and I'll be nearly finished it. They are in the sitting room and sometimes I'll go to my bedroom, but not very often, because my sister and her friend, or boyfriend, will be in there and I think, "Oh God, I may as well go out!" I put it down and I just go out. Then I come back later on. I go to my room and I go to my bed. So I try to do my homework when I know he's not there, at about six o'clock. I put it down when he comes and go out, so I don't really see him.'

Gillian

'If I had a daughter I'd let her have views. She'd have to have manners but I would let her tell me if she thought I'd done something wrong, and why. I can't do that because my mum classes it as disrespect and answering back. A daughter could have her own mind and tell me what she thinks. I'd be more like a friend as well as a mother, whereas my mum's just my mum.

'My family is pretty close really. We have our disagreements but we're pretty close. If anything goes wrong we all stick together and just try to sort it out. My dad's the stronger one. He's always told me that if anyone says something or does something make sure you get on with it yourself and think about how you will deal with it. My mum's very quiet, she'd leave it and tell me to leave it too – try to walk away from it.

'If I have a problem that I want to talk about to do with racism, I find it quite hard to talk to my mum. She'd remind me that my great grandad or grandmother was white. She'd understand my point of view but then she'd try and present me with another point of view.'

Nazrah

'I don't think there was anything wrong with the way that I was brought up, but my mum doesn't really give us any privacy, and if I had a daughter I'd definitely give her some privacy. I'd let her go out more. We're only allowed to go to the library but I'd let her go to the shops, and if she wanted to go to town with a friend that would be all right. My mum puts a lot of restrictions on us, say for example if there's a strike at school, she will want to come and pick us up in the car. My dad would say, "No, come by bus" and then we can have more time with our friends. If there's a school trip my mum will say we can go as a family instead, but my dad will say, "Let them go with their friends and have some fun."'

Erica

'My mum gives me enough freedom considering she didn't have much herself. Her mum died when she was twelve and she had to look after the house and everything because she was the oldest. She had to get up at half six and make grandad's sandwiches for work and then she had to come home and cook. She's given me a lot considering she didn't get a lot. When I'm going out she wants to know who I'm going with and when I'll be back. That's fair. Any mother might expect that.'

7:
Worlds apart

All but one of the girls involved in *Speaking Out* were themselves born in Britain, but they all have one or both parents born abroad, which gives them access to personal sources of information about other places.

Some of the girls had travelled to the Indian subcontinent or to the Caribbean to visit family and all had talked to their parents or grandparents about these places. They were not totally dependent for information on the glossy travel brochures, the newspaper stories, the television series, the news broadcasts, or on the many other indirect sources which help us form our images of other places.

In this discussion, the girls talked about how their family connections influence the way they see the world.

Mumtaz

Mumtaz's parents come from Pakistan where her father was a pilot in the air force. He came to Britain first and worked as a guard on the railway; Mumtaz's mother joined him once he had established a home and a future for them both here. At first she worked as a teacher, teaching Urdu, but then gave up work to look after her children.

Mumtaz is the third child in the family. They are Muslims. She describes her family as close; she says that her life revolves around them. Mumtaz enjoys gardening and is fond of houseplants. She enjoys sports, especially badminton and rounders, which she sometimes plays at home in the garden with her brothers and sisters. Her other interest is reading, mostly fiction.

Recently Mumtaz's father lost his job as a guard, the job he had been doing for some twenty years. Mumtaz explained that this has changed things in the family and affected everyone. They are a large family but have no other relatives in this country and so they rely on each other heavily.

Mumtaz's eldest sister is studying for her A levels at the moment and the two girls enjoy discussing politics together and with two of their brothers. Mumtaz has well thought-out views on a number of issues. Her parents encourage all their children to work hard at school:

'My mum carried on with her education, that's why she wants us to do well. She got her O levels over there [in Pakistan]; she knows that even if you have the qualifications it's hard to get a job. Especially over here where there are fewer and fewer jobs. So she makes us work. My father is the same. He came over to Britain for a broader future and he's always telling us how hard times were – in Pakistan more than here – and how they used to have to walk to school barefooted.'

Mumtaz wants to continue her education, study for A levels and then for a degree. She hopes to become a legal executive and then a solicitor. She knows that many people have low expectations of Asian girls:

'I think it makes you more determined because you're growing up in a white society and so you want to be successful because you're almost condemned by everyone else. Because you're Asian it's harder to get jobs. It's harder to get on with other people because they think of you as an outcast. And so you've got to work hard, harder than some of the white people work, just to get along with people, just to get a proper kind of standard job.'

114

Cynthia

Cynthia is the youngest in a large family. Her parents are from Jamaica and last year her mother spent six months there visiting family. When she returned she brought her own mother back with her.

Cynthia lives in Erdington with her parents, her grandmother and those of her brothers and sisters who have not yet left home. As the youngest she is often subject to teasing and to much well-meaning advice from her sisters. Her family are Christians and members of the New Testament church, and as Cynthia puts it, "quite strict on religion". She is not allowed to go to the cinema, or to go swimming, as she is expected to keep herself covered up.

She is a popular girl, with many friends, and is very keen on drama. Cynthia hopes to take up acting. She has many relatives abroad, including a brother in Canada, and this influences her thoughts about her future:

'I think I'd like to live in Vancouver. My brother wants me to live in Canada but I haven't really made up my mind. Either that or London, but I'm not staying in Birmingham. Not after the way I've seen them portraying Black people here. I don't think there's much here for Black people. It's everything that's happened over the last year or so since the riots. The government portray us as layabouts but really there's talent out there. Sometimes when I'm in town I hear people playing African drums or see Black people drawing on the pavement. I think that's really nice. There's talent in Birmingham and there's talent in Handsworth, but no one goes out to look for it. We could be successful. I'm not saying that all Black people want to work and do well; of course not. There's good and bad in every nation, but here they pinpoint the bad on the Blacks.'

How do Mumtaz and other girls with parents from the Indian subcontinent view these countries? How is Pakistan portrayed in the media? Nazrah's family are preparing to move to Pakistan. In what ways does she expect her life there to be different? What images do Cynthia and other girls hold about Jamaica and the rest of the Caribbean? Does having parents and grandparents who were brought up in another country increase their understanding of world events and world issues? Does it affect their view of Britain's relationships with other countries?

Pakistan

Afia

'Our headteacher went to see a photography exhibition in the Central Library about Pakistan. She said that over here we get a picture of Pakistan which is really of a dusty desert-like place but after she saw the photographs she said that it's beautiful, with a great archaeological heritage. She was going on and on about it and saying how much she'd like to go. The problem is that most people share that view of Pakistan as an unattractive, poor place.'

Nazrah

'There are problems there. People are very ready to take money to do favours. In other words, bribery. I think that's what's really spoiling Pakistan. Here it's not like that. People wouldn't give money to a teacher to pass an examination, but there it can happen, it often does happen. That's what's spoiling Pakistan.'

Afia

'Pakistan is a really nice place but it's also got a bad side. It's the same as England, it's got its good and its bad points. It's just sad that the images on television show the slums and all the problems and not much else. That's why there are people in school, both teachers and girls, who think it's really awful. I've heard people say how horrible it must be to live there in this great desert. They've got the wrong idea.'

Nazrah

'I went in 1985 and my sister and I thought it would be just dust. When we went there it was really green. The roads are dusty but there were some really nice modern places and some massive houses.'

Afia

'I've been there twice, once when I was three and once six years ago. But I can still remember a lot. My grandparents have got a really nice house, a kind of bungalow. They took us out to lovely big gardens. It's a really nice place to live, a bit like the posh areas in Britain, but with less hassle.'

Nazrah

'I don't think that we'll be disappointed with Pakistan when we move there because it's a developing country and things are changing there every single day. I'm going to have to work really hard in school because the students there will be at a more advanced level, and I'll obviously have extra homework. I'll have to calm down, not be so loud, my sister always says I'm a bit mad. I'll have to change in that way and I'll have to change my way of thinking. At home we're mostly ourselves, but when we go out we have to be more disciplined. News travels fast and in Pakistan we'll have to think more about our behaviour. In Asian families reputation counts for a lot. It's the first thing, so when we move to Pakistan we'll have to conduct ourselves in a way that can't be criticized. I'll have to grow my hair, and try and be more ladylike and help my mum more in the house. Even though we'll have people hired to help I'll have to do a bit. I'm bound to find it difficult because nothing changes overnight. We'll have to take it step by step, all of us together. We'll have to stick together, whatever happens, but we do that now. If there's trouble of any sort, if there's a fight, we always stick together as a family.'

Rasheeda

'My parents don't want me to read [go on to higher education]; well my dad says I can, but not my mum. I don't think that's right because we're living here and we should have the choice. I said to my dad, "Look, we're living here so let me read, otherwise let's go to Pakistan. What are we doing here? We are just living here and depending on decisions made about our lives by the British government. We are relying on what they do, so let's go back to Pakistan, our own country, and do everything there."'

Mumtaz

'People from Pakistan don't get news of what's going on in Britain unless it's something really drastic. They don't know the problems of living here. They don't know about the racism they are going to face. They may come here for higher education, hoping to live more comfortably. Unless they have relations here living in an average situation, who write and tell them what it's like, they come thinking that they'll be able to get a job, get married, raise a family and have a stable standard of living. But it's all wrong. There are strict immigration laws which may prevent them coming into the country in the first place. Even people with a right to be here, coming to join their family, may have to wait indefinitely. There are hardly any houses, I don't know about jobs. There are very few good ones and you've got to be really, really qualified to have one. They can't often go to newcomers. They get totally the wrong idea. Someone ought to tell them what it's really like. If the truth came out and Britain ever needed immigrant labour in the future no one would come and the country would go downhill straightaway.'

India

Satnam

'White British people have a picture of India as just dirty. The India they show on telly, it's all dirty, with women in rags. It's not all like that but that's all they show. They show the bad parts of India, not any of the good. Bombay, you get a completely different image of that city from the films they make there. I'm sure a lot of that is idealized, and that it's not like in the films, but at least that's an alternative picture.

'Another aspect of the problem is the way they show Indian people, whether here or in India. A recent example was about an incident in Kent. The first item on the news was about the election. I'm not saying that's unimportant, but it was nothing central, just a politician visiting a factory or something like that. Then they showed a fight in Kent, an item about Sikhs, and it was only on for about two or three seconds near the end of the news. No information was given about the background, no explanation of the situation between Sikhs and other religions in India, so you can imagine the impression people would have got about Sikhs. Violent. Nothing else is shown about the Sikh community so people get their image from this one incident.'

Tara

'I have a very young memory of India. I think of it as home in a way because I remember staying there as a small child for a holiday, just before I started school. I remember taking lots of toys with me. I had a doll that could walk, and when you used to lie her down her eyes would shut. My cousins were all amazed because they'd never seen a doll like that. I can remember a crowd being round me. I left all my things there in New Delhi and when I was little I used to think that I would go back there to get them. I know a little about India from my nan, she's told me about the Hindu gods. I haven't been told a lot but I know they say it's a good place. My sister wants to go because she has never been, but when my nan mentions mosquitoes she says she's changed her mind!'

Jasbir

'I know a bit about India because my parents and family are often talking about it. My mum and all her family used to live in Kenya, in Nairobi. They used to speak Swahili there. My mum went to India to be married, as did some of her sisters. They lived there for a while before coming to England. My granny really hates Birmingham and England, she doesn't like the weather. Mum really wants to go to India. She hasn't been there for over twenty years. We were planning on going as a family but it doesn't look like that will happen. My sister went about three years ago with my dad and my granny. My gran's been in and out of India a few times.'

Erica

'We had a girl in our class who had lived in Kenya, an Asian girl, and when people knew that she'd lived in Africa they would ask such stupid questions. They were surprised she could speak English for a start. It was so embarrassing. They thought that people walked around there in grass skirts with no tops on. She told them she'd never seen anyone walking around like that and that people were properly dressed! Africa, Jamaica, it's all the same in some of their minds.'

Jamaica

Marcia

'I hear quite a lot about Jamaica from my mum, but not from my dad because he doesn't keep in regular touch with those of his brothers and sisters that are still in Jamaica. My mum's got a big family and most of them live in Jamaica. My mum was born in St Elizabeth and she's planning to go back next summer because she hasn't been for about ten years. You need a lot of money in Jamaica. To get there costs enough. Once you're there the Jamaicans expect you to have a lot of money because you're living in England. They expect you to bring them all presents. My mum remembers lots of little kids swarming around her when she went back, hoping for presents and talking about how they would love to come over here. She spent most of the day going up into the town and it was so hot that you didn't need to wear shoes on the way. Half the time there's no need to buy fruit because where my nan lives they've got oranges, bananas and mangoes. My mum said one of the things she liked best about Jamaica was the beach. I feel I know the place because my mum talks so much about it. I'm glad she does.'

Cynthia

'Last year my mum stayed for six months in Jamaica. She came back and brought my nan over as well. So my nan's in England now. My mum does go on about it but she prefers England to Jamaica. The whole family got together and we sorted out stuff to send to Jamaica. Everybody over there thought she had millions of pounds. We had this massive trunk we shipped there and it arrived about four weeks after my mum arrived. It was supposed to be for the family but everybody heard and came round. She felt really bad because she didn't have something for everybody. She's got a lot of family in Jamaica, Canada and America. Most of my mum's family is in either Jamaica or London. I'd love to travel. I'd like to go to Africa and to see Canada and Jamaica.'

Gillian

'I can't really say where I'd like to end up. I like Jamaica but you also have to have the money. It isn't bad on my mum's side because they have the money where they live in St Ann's Bay. When I was over there I had my own horse, I had everything that I wanted. When I went over to my dad's family it was totally different. You just have to face up to the few things that you've got, because it's so expensive out there. When I was living in America there were places I liked and there were places I didn't like. We lived in Ohio and in Brooklyn. I think it's different for Black people in the States than it is in Britain. In America there's racism but Black people over there know where they stand.'

Apart from the Indian subcontinent and the Caribbean, the two areas of the world from which the parents and grandparents of the girls had migrated, the two other places the girls most wanted to discuss were South Africa and the United States. South Africa and the injustices of apartheid were frequent themes, whether the starting point of the conversation had been school or other parts of the world. Many of the girls had strong views on the power of the United States in world affairs, on Britain's relationship with America, and on nuclear weapons.

South Africa

Satnam
'South Africa is somewhere I don't really feel I know enough about. They don't show as much as I'd like them to on the news. I don't think it's right what's happening, I don't think it's right at all.'

Marcia
'People should realize what's going on. They are not showing the things that are happening because they shouldn't be happening. The South African government have put a ban on television news and on filming. Even so there is a clear picture of what's going on: Black people are slaving away for the

government in South Africa and they are not getting anything for it. They've got no rights.

'I think that everybody who's against apartheid should learn more about South Africa; just go through and research more about it. That's the only way we're going to be able to do something by finding out more about it and from that we can suggest what to do. It's going to be hard because it's not our country, but there will be things we can do to support those who are fighting apartheid there. Something can be done if we just take the trouble to look and think clearly. It's difficult to get people concerned because they are not seeing it on the television except when they are giving news which is about some other aspect. The news isn't really dealing with it. When it comes to apartheid you're not seeing anything.'

Jasbir
'It's so stupid: everyone is a human being so they should all have the same rights. It doesn't matter what colour you are. You should be treated the same. There's no reason for it all.'

Trade boycott

Marcia
'I heard that they are building another shop selling South African clothes in town so they don't care do they? They sell South African goods and if the shop's there people just buy. They just don't care. For most people South Africa is just another thing. Another idea here, another idea there, and just throw it aside. But it isn't just something else! The government has got to sit up and look at it!'

Tara
'I agree with Jasbir. We should be trying to support the Black people in South Africa. We should be trying to help each other. We should stop buying all the South African goods.'

Gillian

'If the government wanted to do something about it they would. You can guarantee they don't want to do anything about it. If they did they'd stop importing South African goods. Then the South Africans would have to stop because they would have no resources. The government haven't stopped imports from South Africa mainly because Margaret Thatcher and her friends have got millions of pounds invested in South Africa so she'll obviously not stop else she'll lose out. And it's the same with other countries. It's only a few countries that will sacrifice that and they are first of all the other Black countries. They say it's their brother country so they will help. There's a lot more Europe and America could do to help but they just won't do it. The majority of people just don't care. They think, there's Black people . . . and done.'

Get involved!

Cynthia

'It's worth getting involved, campaigning outside shops and so on, so you can tell people what they are doing. There are probably people walking around town buying those things who don't even know that they are South African. I was talking to a girl and she didn't know, she'd bought some clothes and she didn't know they were South African. She said she'll never go there again. If you decide to campaign outside a shop you know there would be trouble but it will tell some people what's going on.'

Marcia

'Things like the sale of goods just go quietly without anyone noticing. That's why, if no one makes publicity, then South Africa will just go on strengthening itself. The more wealthy they get the stronger force they will be. But if I was to organize a campaign, I'd go round schools and anywhere and tell them more about apartheid in South Africa.

'One thing that would really hurt all these shops – I got this idea from Brookside – is to put up slogans across the front of the shops. You could say:"You're killing off niggers! Do you like it?" Unless you use strong language like that you won't touch people. Language like that shows that it hurts you to think about it and forces them to think about it.

'I saw a programme about South Africa, well, not even a programme, a clipping. They showed the white people in houses and the Black people in little hutches. And it's the Black people who are doing all the work. They keep moving them about the country wherever they need them to work and all the money they make goes back to the white people. It's so wrong. That's why I'm totally against it.'

Gillian

'They don't really care about Black people, neither here nor there. Our government don't want to apply sanctions because they'll hurt themselves. I'd better cut down because things like this really hurt me and just make me angry. They are protecting their own. When I think how Black people are treated . . . not even Black people . . . when I think how people are treated, could be Black or white, it would still hurt. Why should people be treated that way?'

American problem

Nazrah

'I think the world's big problem is America. It wants to be part of everything. And all the wars that are going on, it's none of their business, but they're still poking their noses in. It's in the Middle East that the superpowers are interested in influencing what's going on. Wars sometimes worry us in a personal way because we've got friends all over the world and we're mostly thinking of them.'

Mumtaz

'I think the main cause is America. The Russians come into it as well, but I think the Americans are the main problem in the world. If there was no America then most of the problems would be solved. They have a lot of nuclear weapons that influence other countries like Britain, and they get involved in wars between other countries like Iran and Iraq and I think they just do everything wrong. They give people bad ideas about other places. I don't think we should listen to them. They have a big influence on Britain and on Margaret Thatcher. As she's Prime Minister it involves us all.

   'They play on people's fear of foreigners and of other different countries. For example, with Gaddafi, and the war and the terrorists, everyone thought that every Arab was a terrorist. But that's only because America made it out to be like that. They said that Gaddafi is a terrorist and that all the people who follow him are terrorists. They just left it at that. But there are real people involved. America would rather you believe that they are all terrorists and leave it like that.'

Nuclear fear

Afia

'I think what Nazrah is saying about America is true but I think America and England are a problem together. Thatcher agrees with everything that the Americans say and I think that's a bit stupid. You've got to have your own views on certain things. The prospect of nuclear war is really frightening because it will affect us and it will affect the next generations too. What will they think about the world? It's just wars and it's gradually deteriorating. Nuclear war really frightens me because I think, "When I grow up I'm going to have a future" but the future is just the war isn't it? It looks as though in the 1990s the world will have more, not less, nuclear weapons.'

Mumtaz
'Nuclear war, unemployment, they are both important issues, because with unemployment what will become of the country? But nuclear war, everyone dreads that because it will affect everybody. It's silly that they've got the weapons in the first place.'

Rasheeda
'America's only got nuclear weapons because Russia's got them, then Russia will get more and then so will America. If they want to fight let them fight, but they should do it without all these weapons that affect everyone else. It's simply about competition – who can be the one who can most effectively blow up the world? Put them somewhere where they can fight on their own without these things.

'When I see wars going on I think they are fighting with other countries, but soon they'll get here. What I'm really worried about is that it might affect me before I even get a chance to be an adult. I'll probably die before that time.'

Afia
'We mustn't have a nuclear war. People vote for Thatcher or Kinnock or whoever, and the people in America vote for Reagan but I don't think they should play with people's lives and assume it's a big game. They don't have the right to blow us up.'

Nazrah
'Thatcher just wants to stay on America's good side, so that if there is war we can go to America for help. Britain hasn't got

many nuclear weapons, America and Russia are leading, so if Britain is in trouble she hopes America will become involved.'

World peace . . . an impossible dream?

Mumtaz

'It's difficult to stop it all now because these weapons are made and you can't get rid of them. Even if you dump them somewhere they're still around. The technology is still around. While they exist there's always the danger that the whole world can be destroyed. As one country's government makes more bombs then the other countries make more and you get a whole pile of nuclear bombs ready to use.'

Nazrah

'I blame America. They started it all, and they just bring every other country into it. The arms deal they had with Iran for example. They're selling the arms and encouraging smaller countries to try and keep up with them, and no country wants to be at war with America because they know they're so much bigger and stronger.'

Afia

'I think the prospect of world peace is impossible now because powerful countries have so much pride. They think, "Why should we get rid of the weapons?" and to get world peace you have to agree. The governments of so many countries have to agree. Apartheid for instance, they've got to get rid of that before they can get on to the prospect of nuclear war. But with apartheid everybody was saying to Mrs Thatcher, "Why don't you do something?" but she didn't want to do anything. Black people are suffering and many are getting killed. If it were white people who were suffering she'd do something about it straight away.'

Wealth equals power

Afia

'There shouldn't really be any poor countries in the world or any poor people, but I don't think you can stop it because the greedy countries like America just want the best for themselves. They put on a front that they are helping other countries but they are not really, they are just making matters worse. We just take what we want from these countries, like coffee for instance, and pay them very little for it. All these groups that try to help poor countries, the Red Cross for instance, all they can do is help in a crisis but they can't really stop the poverty without taking away power from the rich. America has got more power because of its technology. Relatively few people are poor there. The North has a lot more power and has nuclear weapons.'

Mumtaz

'I don't think there should be famine, not in the 1980s and 1990s. America, England and all the other rich countries should get together and do something about it. With Live Aid and Band Aid it took pop stars to do something. There was this Tory MP who said, "Well, pop stars should do something about it, it doesn't just depend on us." But they are in power, they form the government, they have a responsibility to do something. If they are going to say that why don't they let the pop stars run the government?'

Nazrah

'The problem is that we don't know enough about it. We are taught about the people in these countries who have brought famine on themselves. We hear that their ancestors have ruined the land, so we think all they need to learn about is land cultivation. I've never heard anyone explain that rich countries may help maintain the poverty of these countries by buying goods at cheap prices. They certainly have never mentioned it in school. We just learn about the physical things to do with the earth. We don't think about what countries might be doing to each other. They'd say it would be too controversial and there would be quarrelling in class.'

Mumtaz

'In school you don't try to look at the whole world and think about relationships. In geography you look at a country or region and that's mostly it. For example, at the moment we're looking at West Africa. But we ought to think about the whole world because famine can't just be blamed on the people and the land and on natural causes. You can spoil a whole country if you have trade sanctions. If you stop trading you can bring down a whole economy. The relationships between countries are important. Like America doesn't do anything about stopping trade with South Africa and influences Britain to do nothing. One country is influencing another and the second one should really have its own opinion, but it can't because it's not so strong. The smaller countries do what the powerful ones do. They follow the others.'

False picture

Rasheeda

'On TV they show developing countries as poor, they make out the people are lazy, or not exactly lazy but not too bothered about anything, perhaps because of the weather and the heat. They suggest that that makes them feel like not working. I think they should go into it more. They should look more closely at a country's economy and those sort of things rather than show pictures of starving children, Black starving children in particular.'

130

Afia

'People here, when they see the starving children, they think, "Oh, it's children starving! How terrible! We'd better be kind to them. We'd better help them!" They are not thinking about the country's relationships. They are not thinking about the way they vote.

'I don't think it's the responsibility of people like Bob Geldof to make their minds up for them. I don't think he should do that because it's not his job, and he says that himself. He's just pointing out that you should look at who you're voting for. Look at the countries. Think about famine.'

Mumtaz

'I don't think that half the pop stars were really bothered about what they were raising money for. They just thought, "This will be a good image-maker for ourselves. We'll look really kind and generous and we can gain some more fans by playing live." There were some sincere ones but half of them don't know what they are there for. So they can't put it to proper use.'

Afia

'I don't think we get a very true picture. We see poor countries and people get the impression that the whole country is a desert. ITV and the BBC, they are restricted because they are trying to find pictures that will make people really look at the news. The whole thing is so restricted. I don't know if it's true or not but it was said with the Falklands war that the Prime Minister had to approve the news in some way. If we see the news through Margaret Thatcher's eyes we're not going to understand the vital parts of it.'

Conclusion:
Making changes

■■■

The girls who contributed to *Speaking Out* discovered that sharing experiences, ideas and feelings is a way of giving and receiving support. One of the first steps we can take to bring about changes in our lives is to talk about the issues which concern us.

Satnam
'I found it really interesting talking to the other girls. Take Marcia and Gillian for example. They've not got exactly the same life as me, but it is similar in that they've got problems and worries and so have I. It's easier after talking, because I know I'm not in it alone. I've learnt to get closer to them.'

In the introduction to this book Afia said that "girls must learn to stand up for themselves". Standing up for ourselves and for each other is another step towards change which women in many communities are taking.

Nazrah
'The men have known that they can take advantage of the women because they've always thought they are not going to quarrel and answer back as much as men. That's why men have tried to push more and more on to women. But women are changing, and we should change. I think it's happening in all sorts of cultures and that's how it should be. It's happening among the Asian community in Britain, and it's happening among women in Pakistan.

'Take Benazir Bhutto. She's got crowds behind her now. I really admire her, she's done a lot for women by taking her stand. She must have worked hard with just a small number of supporters to begin with. But she's determined to do things in a democratic way, building up votes, and changing her country for the better.'

Throughout this book the girls discussed issues of justice and injustice which touch the daily lives of Black people in Britain. But they also argued that international issues: the relationship between rich countries and developing countries; between countries like Britain and America; the situation in South Africa; media images of the West Indies, Africa and the Indian subcontinent should be everyone's concern. They showed how these issues affect attitudes towards Black people in Britain and how, by finding out about what is happening in the world, Black girls can begin to challenge racism at school and in society generally. The girls talked about the need to think about the relationships between countries, rather than just assuming that poor nations have brought hardship or famine on themselves. They spoke about campaigning, suggesting that one way of getting involved is simply to talk to people about what is going on.

Of course it's easy to feel strongly about things which are happening in the world but to feel rather powerless to do anything about them. If we do speak out, how will teachers and parents respond?

Rasheeda
'Some teachers will be taken aback when they read what we think. Some of them will think that we will say these things and then give up. They'll think that Asian girls will say they want to do certain things but that the struggle won't be worth it. I think they'll be surprised when we actually go ahead and do what we want to do with our lives.'

Afia

'My mum knows me. She knows what my views are, and she knows she can trust me, so I think she'll support what I'm saying. But my dad is in for a shock when he eventually realizes that his daughter is not what he expected her to be.'

Cynthia

'My mum thinks it's good that we've had the chance to talk about these things. She thinks it's good that we can feel free to actually talk about issues like racism together, and to see what we can do with our own lives.'

The girls were all agreed that the subjects they had discussed are relevant to all young women, both Black and white. Although they admitted that they would find some subjects difficult to discuss in front of white girls they looked forward to hearing how other girls would respond:

Erica

'No white girls took part in our discussions, and I sometimes wished that one or two were there so I could hear what they had to say. I'll be interested to know what the ones that aren't racist have to say about the things we've been talking about. I'm looking forward to hearing their views.'

Nazrah

'I'm sure that all Black girls will recognize something in what we've been saying. Black girls will see how we see racism and prejudice and they'll compare their experiences with ours.

'I hope white people will read this. They'll find out what Asian girls and Afro-Caribbean girls think of them, and of this country. They'll see we've got views on plenty of other issues too. I hope they'll start seeing something of what we can see, and get a trace of what our lives are like.'

Other Virago Upstart

My Love, My Love or The Peasant Girl

Rosa Guy

Rosa Guy's deceptively simple retelling of Andersen's tale, 'The Little Mermaid', is set on a lush and beautiful Caribbean island. Desirée Dieu-Donné, a poor peasant girl, rescues and falls in love with the handsome son of a rich family. Bargaining with the gods for his life, she pledges her own, defying all the taboos of race and class to be by his side. But she is not of his world, and her fate is inevitable – and tragic.

Rosa Guy was born in Trinidad and grew up in New York. Virago publishes her adult novel, *A Measure of Time*.

Bitter-Sweet Dreams

Girls' and Young Women's Own Stories

By the readers of *Just Seventeen*

'It's about time you let us have our say.' This reply from a Merseyside girl was echoed by teenagers across Britain who responded to Virago's invitation in *Just Seventeen* magazine to paint a picture of what their lives are like. The result is riveting and sobering. Consuming details of daily life – exams and jobs, clothes and friends – contrast with their own cautionary tales of young mothers, drugs and restless lives. Family and love dominate, and faced with the reality of unemployment, many write longingly of their desire for 'a brilliant career'. Clear-eyed, plain-speaking, wistful yet knowing, here are the bitter-sweet dreams of the eighties generation.

Send a S.A.E. for our complete list.